WHAT READERS LOVE ABOUT *HANNIBAL'S WITCH*

"Absolutely fascinating!

"This was a most interesting story, with a realistic view of someone who might actually travel to the past, who thinks through the consequences of her actions, knowing that she will change history and cause billions of people to not be born. Angela knows what the "real" history is (e.g. who wins what battles) and was torn between helping Rome succeed with its conquests by force and admittedly great advances in engineering, and helping Carthage succeed with its spread of civilization by voluntary trade. It was hard to put it down. Very intriguing plot twists. It make me think what it would be like to be in her place to use my current knowledge to 'guide' the course of history."

"Captivating and riveting! Very well written story that brings to life an alternative world if Rome was not the conqueror. Can one person really change history? Should you even if you could? Once I started into the story, I couldn't put it down. A good blend of history and philosophy woven into an adventure of a lifetime."

I0593324

TITLES BY ROBIN CRAIG

The Hunter Series

Frankensteel

The Geneh War

Time Enough for Killing

Leonardo's Child

Time Travel and Alternative History

The Time Surgeons

Hannibal's Witch

The Passion of Judas

Short Stories

Past, Present Future

Non-Fiction Philosophy

Dialogue on the Two Chief World Systems

Good Without God

Cloning Around: The Ethics of Human Cloning and Stem Cell
Research

For the latest news visit robin-craig.com or follow on
fb.me/authorcraig

Hannibal's Witch

ROBIN CRAIG

Published by ThoughtWare Books.

Available from Amazon.com and other retail outlets.
Available on Kindle and other devices.

This book is a work of fiction. Except for historical facts, any resemblance to people or corporations, living or dead, is entirely coincidental.

Cover art by Kira Craig using images from Pixabay with fonts from 1001 Fonts.

Author's website: robin-craig.com

Printed Version ISBN 978-0-9803205-3-4

What is history? An echo of the past in the future; a reflex from the future on the past. — Victor Hugo

CONTENTS

ACKNOWLEDGEMENTS

My thanks go to historian Dr Michael Affleck and members of the Quora community (with special thanks to B. Wolfe, E. J. Brennan and M. A. Hall) for their insights into aspects of ancient Rome and the difficulties Hannibal faced against the Romans, though any historical errors remain mine. My wife Sonja gave me the idea for this book with her Phoenician "what ifs" and tales of the world of bitcoin. My brother Stuart's under-appreciated assessment of war also found its place in here.

Carthago Delenda Est

I am a philosopher.

Who are the immortals, do you think? Are they the conquerors, who lay waste to so many lives and cities, and build their glory on the bodies of others? Or do you think they are the kings and emperors, who rule over their lands with bronze and iron?

No. It is the philosophers who are immortal. Who else create the thoughts which transform the minds and souls of men, and whose writings may continue to change them as long as people live and breathe on this Earth? They may struggle and be forgotten, yet even then their thoughts may reach other minds, and so some fragment of their souls live on. Perhaps the works of the greatest of them, giants like Aristotle, will live forever; and even millennia hence men will study their words and be amazed at the minds that formed them for the first time.

Do you ask who I am? My name does not matter. Nobody will remember me. For as much as I am a philosopher, I am also a slave. But what defines a man? The accidents of birth or life? How those around him see him? No. What defines a man is how he defines himself. What a man chooses to think in the sanctuary of his own mind can never be taken away.

So today I am a slave, scribe to the Roman general Scipio Aemilianus, writing his letters and recording his mighty deeds. And today I am a philosopher, bearing witness to the death of greatness.

Sometimes greatness drifts away and no one can say for certain when it crosses the border from greatness into obscurity, like a man slowly dying from a wound that cannot heal. But other times men can look upon the end of greatness and mark the exact day.

These people call themselves Canaani, for their ancestors came from the land of Canaan on the eastern shore of the Great Sea. But to the rest of us they are the Phoenicians: the people of purple. For that is the origin of their power and wealth. Others before them had known of the rich purple dye that could be extracted from sea snails, a dye that brightened rather than faded in the sun. But it is the Phoenicians who turned it into an art and an industry, and on that they built their empire.

Before the Persians and their vast empire, before Alexander of Macedon who would rule the world, the Phoenicians had an empire which stretched from west to east and north to south across the Great Sea at the center of the world.

An empire built on snails.

But more than snails and the purple treasure buried inside them. They traded in everything that men and women might desire: the finest wood and glass, metals and more. With them they carried culture, and philosophy, and art. Even the papyrus on which I write they traded throughout the world, so much so that their great city Byblos, the oldest city in the world, was named for it. But greater than the papyrus on which men write, they brought their alphabet to do the writing. And from that first alphabet came all others, including the alphabet of the Romans who have destroyed them.

Rome is not the first. Their homeland was conquered by the Persians. Their great city Tyre, thinking itself safe in its island fortress, spurned Alexander, but still it fell to the victory lust of he who would never be denied. But their empire stretched across the world and one of their seeds, planted far away on the shore of Africa, grew to become mighty Carthage, so great that even the Romans had grown to fear it.

First they fought the Romans in Sicily, and lost, and were impoverished. Yet they rose again, and a generation later their greatest general, Hannibal, brought his army into Italy itself and there struck fear into Roman hearts, crushing their armies time and time again. For fifteen long years Hannibal tormented Italy, but final victory eluded him. Then the great Roman general Scipio Africanus attacked Carthage itself, luring Hannibal home, and there at last Hannibal met his match.

What is it about Rome, that they must rule the world? Once they were just another city in Italy, surrounded by many other peoples: the Etruscans, Sabines, Latins, Samnites and Volsci to name but some.

Now they command all Italy. My own people, the Greeks, who in past ages took Troy, bloodied the mighty Persians, and gave birth to Alexander the Great: now even they are falling before Rome, if they have not already fallen.

And Rome would not forget Carthage. And so two generations after Hannibal the drumbeats began:

Carthago delenda est.

Carthage must be destroyed.

The sentiment was not original, but that particular drumbeat was pounded by Cato the Wise, indeed so often that perhaps it will become his epitaph. Cato was just a youth when Hannibal first entered Italy, and his enmity against Carthage came to match Hannibal's against Rome. Thus is hate handed from generation to generation and nation to nation. From Hamilcar to Hannibal to Cato. From the Scipio nearly killed by Hannibal to his son who defeated Hannibal to his great grandson, the man who came here dragging me in his wake. That is why, a scant three years later, I am here to witness the death of Carthage.

A ragged line of women and children trudge past me on their way to slavery, their empty eyes seeing nothing, not even a future. What hopes and dreams did they have just a few years before today? Now their husbands and fathers are dead and their dreams have become dust. We can never see the future, and I wonder if we would want to if we could, or if the first sight of it would send us running back to trembling blindness.

But we never stop trying to see the future, and I wonder if that is our glory or our curse. My people are gone. Carthage is gone. Now nothing stands in the way of Rome and her unlimited ambition. I wonder if one day the Romans will own the whole world.

As I look out upon the glow of the last fires of Carthage, I wonder what they will do with it when they do.

Chapter 1: The Monastery

The party is in full swing when I arrive.

Had you asked me a year ago for the most unlikely venue for a party, let alone a party I would be invited to, 'monastery' probably would not have been on the list. Not because I would have thought it likely, but because it is so unlikely I never would have thought of it at all.

I smile at the irony. I do not believe in God. If you showed me God and I were forced to believe in Him, I would not believe he is good. I would fear Him—as what sane person would not?—but I would fear him as I would fear any other power able to do to me what He will, with no higher court of appeal to call His caprice to judgement.

But that is not the irony. The irony is that I once believed in God, and not any old God, but the particular one to which this monastery was dedicated. The vengeful God of the Christian Bible. Tamed, some say, in the New Testament of that Bible: less angry, more forgiving and inclusive. If, that is, one thinks it is mellow to move from large scale smiting to killing your own Son because that is the only way you can imagine saving the world from your own Judgement. The Zen Buddhists believe that it is only by contemplating the paradox or the contradictory that one can achieve enlightenment. Perhaps the Christians have merely taken it one step further, and seek enlightenment through contemplation of the insane.

Do you condemn me for these thoughts in this place? For betraying the God whose presence you imagine I should feel all around me in a building dedicated to His worship? Believe what you like, but I tell you it is He who betrayed me. No, I shall not tell you the details. It is enough to say that if the Bible is true, then its God betrayed me; and if it is not true, then His religion is based on nothing but the words of priests. The words of men, not the Word of God. A fiction, not a fact.

I see no need to explain this to you or to justify myself in your eyes. Let us just say that God promised his sheep that no matter how much he tempted or tormented them—what a loving Father He is!— He would never allow them to be tempted beyond their strength to endure. Yet I was tested, and I endured; I was punished, and I prayed; and at the end I was pushed beyond my limits to bear it, and I crumbled.

Do you dare condemn me now? Do you dare blame me for lacking the strength? Well, I tell you that your God is a liar. Your religion calls his adversary the Prince of Lies; I do not believe in this adversary either, but if I did I must ask the question: who is the Liar?

I studied logic once. I am good at it. There are no contradictions in reality, for how can what is contradict what is? Yet here is the contradiction: that God will not test his believers beyond their breaking point, and yet I broke. Therefore the Bible is false. Therefore your God does not exist, or if He does we can claim no knowledge about him and he might as well not.

I have told this story to friends who believe, and they say the flaw lies in me. But when I ask them to prove their God they have no proof. All their arguments from things we can actually see in the reality around us, whether they speak of design or prophecy or revelation, are fallacious: and to build your belief on them is to leave it on a flawed foundation, waiting to crumble. All they are left with is faith: they feel God in their hearts, they say, and thus they know Him, and thus they know he exists. But I say to you: if your feelings show you the truth, how can you dismiss mine? Once I had your feelings, too; now I know I am betrayed. If your feelings are valid, then so are mine. You are the one who believes men can be led astray by some Prince of Lies from another dimension. So perhaps it is you who have been, not I.

In any case we can all agree that God has abandoned this place. I am young but I have travelled. I have visited cathedrals where, if there is a God, His power and presence is manifest in the gold, jewels and soaring beauty they contain.

No, I do not approve of it. As beauty, yes: for who cannot approve of beauty as an abstract ideal? Even if misguided: if its soaring glory reaches for an imaginary Heaven instead of its proper aspiration toward all that is best within us, its builders. But the splendor of a cathedral is a beauty distilled and concentrated from the unsung labor of countless others. They worked and died, donating whatever pennies or gold they could spare from their purses, perhaps to the glory of God, perhaps to pay for their sins real or imagined. And so the veins of the countryside drew in the wealth of those who labored in its fields and mines and waters, concentrating it into golden spires reaching toward a Heaven that does not exist.

Once it must have been the same here, and when faith was stronger or wealth easier to come by, this place grew fat on the sap drawn from its roots in the souls of men. But now! More irony! For did not Jesus cast out the merchants from His temple, deeming them an affront to its holiness? Yet here today we have the monks of this temple, faded in numbers and power, able to hold their shrunken domain only by giving over the rest to us servants of Mammon. If Moses came down from his mountain and saw this, he would name it a celebration of money, and break his tablets in renewed rage and shame to see this is the end of the road he started.

Do you wonder why I stand here amidst a swirl of color and sound, having these thoughts? No more than do I. Perhaps the setting has awaken an old guilt. No, not the guilt of betraying God. The guilt of betraying myself by ever believing in Him.

Have I stood here for minutes, while these thoughts have gone through my head? Or has it been mere moments, the thoughts a summation of the years I have travelled to reach this point? Nobody stares at me, so it must have been moments; or maybe they do not care to look, too involved in this celebration of their own glory. I wonder what the monks, cloistered in their cellars somewhere below, are thinking of us. Do they frown in bitter condemnation of us and their own failure in reaching this end? Or do they lust to join us, to for once let their reins go in a feast of food, liquor and women? Perhaps both, and they will sin in their dreams as much as they imagine we sin in the flesh, and their penance will be as severe as their guilt, even though their guilt is as imaginary as their sins.

Again I wonder how it is I came to be here myself. The mechanism is clear; the causes more murky.

There are signposts in the fog. Me at college. Young, innocent, afire, virginal. Yes, virginal. Even if the words 'virginal' and 'college' rarely cohabit in the one thought. No, it was not that I was never tempted; I merely never allowed the temptation and opportunity to collide. Perhaps that was by intent. Perhaps by unhappy accident. Though back then I would have called it a happy accident, for I wished the secret joys of love to be discovered with the hero God would give me when the time was right, not be squandered too early on a casual pleasure with unworthy lovers. More fool me, I know now. And my body, or perhaps the undeceived portion of my mind, agreed even then. For I knew the delicious feelings in delicious places—as what young person does not?—and often enough felt the urge to bring them to their natural conclusion in the meeting of bodies: if not in true and abiding love, then in honest passion for a mate worthy of at least that much. The monks below celebrate love and condemn lust. But lust is an honor bestowed on its object, just as love is, only an honor from the body rather than the spirit. And why would we condemn such an honor as if our bodies are unworthy of its giving or taking?

But I digress. The first signpost was a boy. I did not know him well. I think he fancied me, but he never intruded much on my thoughts. He was an awkward boy. His dark eyes held a fire that spoke of an arresting intelligence, and I knew he did well in his classes, almost without trying; but when those dark eyes looked into mine all I saw was his awkwardness, and he did not stir any of those delectable tremors in my body. But do not judge me too harshly. I did not laugh at him, to his face or behind his back, as some did at his oddness; I did not despise him. I liked him, though he was too strange for me to call him a close friend. I do not know what friends he did have; I do not know why he did what he did; but he was the first step on my road to this place with its dying monastery below and its exuberant life above. I smile at that image as it enters my mind. Like an inversion of heaven and hell, with the happy sinners celebrating above and the miserable saints moaning beneath. Or is that a reflection of the reality of those two realms?

One day I was sitting on the lawn eating lunch when this boy came to me. He told me of this thing called 'bitcoin'. I knew nothing of it. He, it soon transpired, knew everything. A new form of money, he called it. Instead of money backed by the assertions of government or gold dug from the ground, its value and integrity came from computers. I did not see the point, but I freely admitted I knew little about it. He laughed, though not unkindly. It seems there is a world of difference between what he called 'government money' and money as it used to be, backed by gold, and this was the next evolution in money: one belonging to our technological age where power and wealth lie in knowledge, not guns and shovels. But whilst the evolution from gold to government cut money from its root and validation in real value (not by accident, but by intent), this next evolution would return it to reality. Or so he said.

I hope that after all these years I can do justice to his words. This is how I remember our conversation.

"Government money," he said to me, "is a giant con. What is it based on? Do you even know that our money used to be backed by gold? A real value? That underneath all the pieces of paper we swap around was the guarantee that if you needed or wanted to, you could take those pieces of paper to a bank and get back their value in gold, real, tangible gold?"

"But… it seems to work," I replied. "Why, these days, half the time we don't even use the pieces of paper. I put a piece of plastic in a machine, or type its number into a web form."

"It works because everyone trusts it. But there have been many occasions when the government has defaulted, when hit by reality or just to achieve some end of their own, and it has become worthless. Even our own government prints money when they want to. They claim they are managing the economy. What they are doing is eroding the value of your savings as a form of indirect taxation."

"But if the government can just print money and tell us what it's worth, how can it crash like you say?"

"They can't really just print it and declare its value. They claim they can, but that's part of the con. It is really based on the production of the country. That's where its value comes from. Worse, when the government runs on debt as it often does, its value is a mortgage on future production. In essence it is a kind of pyramid scheme, based on never running out of new producers still willing to work hard to create the value it depends upon. Sometimes, whether because of war or just bad management, it does run out of producers. Then it crashes."

"So what's this got to do with this 'bitcoin' you told me about?"

"Bitcoin is decentralized—in theory it can be spread all around the world, beyond country borders—and based on computing power. A problem with gold is that as technology gets better, more and more gold gets produced. So far, though it fluctuates with supply, demand

and speculation about supply and demand, that has managed to track our actual productivity: the amount of gold we can mine is set by the level of our technology and wealth. But bitcoin is inherently linked to the power of our technology, which underpins our entire economy. So it has objective value, without government meddling, without central planning, without borders!"

I am not an economist. I cannot say whether he was right or wrong. I know plenty of people agree with him while plenty of others don't. I have gained enough affinity with his cynical views to suspect the motives of those who disagree, living as they usually do off cream skimmed from the system they so stoutly defend. But I know when to make no conclusions.

What I also know is that he advised me to buy some of this bitcoin. It was new, he said. But it was the wave of the future. As more people saw its value, its 'exchange rate' with real money (how cross he would be if he heard me call it that!) would grow. If I bought some now it could bring me great returns; perhaps even make me comfortably well off.

I was hesitant, as you can imagine. I was a student and my family was not wealthy. I had no interest in speculative investment, so I demurred. He rejoined that even something little, like a hundred dollars, could end up paying for a new car or at least a grand holiday just a few years down the track. He was so sure that he would even give me the money, if I promised to spend it on bitcoin.

I admit I was somewhat taken aback! Why would he be so generous? What was I to him? I looked at his eager face, so full of his own excitement about his 'wave of the future', and wondered. I might have been a virgin but I was not ignorant. I knew boys: if I had not, my misfortune in so far escaping the joys of sexual passion would have ended long ago, for few things make boys more cunning than the chance of exploring desired flesh. So I knew that the shiny baubles boys offered often contained a hook and a price. Why did I think this boy was any different? I had never thought of my friend, if friend he was, in that light, and the thought gave me pause. His physical type was not the kind that generally evoked temptations in my flesh, though he was not unattractive. Should I be ashamed that I was so shallow? He was odd, but he was interesting and I have already noted his intellect, which is even more attractive in a man than well cut biceps—or, should I say, should be. Then I knew that if I accepted his gift, I would be drawn into his sphere of influence. Sooner rather than later, perhaps after a drink in celebration or commiseration over our investment's progress, the delicious feeling would come and I would fall from God's grace into a man's arms and be lost.

How cheap would I be, to sell my honor for a hundred dollars? I wished to follow Jesus, not Judas. But I was not angry. Perhaps this temptation lay only in my own craven flesh, while his heart was pure and generous! So I smiled, told him he was sweet, but that I could not accept such a gift. He frowned a moment, then leapt to his feet with a smile. Perhaps those dark eyes had read my soul, and he was amused. I remember his words. They were simply, "I understand! But remember my words: it costs so little! What do you have to lose?"

Then he was gone.

Second signpost. I did consider his words. I realized he was right: one hundred dollars was an amount I could afford to lose—I mean invest!—and perhaps on this occasion I should act on his intellect and knowledge rather than on my own cautious ignorance.

"Live a little!" I thought to myself. As have how many gamblers throughout history, to their ultimate chagrin? And having once allowed such recklessness into my heart, I threw caution to the winds and invested double.

And he was right. Two hundred dollars hurt me only psychologically, not physically. Perhaps I bought one or two fewer nice meals or items of clothing. I do not remember, and that says it all, does it not?

He was also wrong. Third signpost. I never cashed in my bitcoins for a new car or a cruise around the Mediterranean. My attitude to investment was what I considered wisdom: if you are worried about losing it, don't do it. Ideally, don't care whether you lose it or not. I had started with the former but let myself be persuaded by the urging of an odd but brilliant man; I ended with the latter, when I never missed the morsel I had spent.

My forgetting was aided by the fourth signpost. My life had entered a period of traumatic change, and money I did not miss was soon forgotten.

If you recall my thoughts about religion, you might be surprised at what I had been studying. Perhaps it would have led me to this very place via a quite different route. For what I had been studying was theology. With my false love of God and my true love of logic, it was a reasonable choice. In it I discovered my happy coincidence of both interest and skill in languages.

The logic that led me there was clear. If God was real, and He revealed Himself to us through His Word, then we can only understand Him through that Word. But the Word was not written in English or any other modern language: it was revealed in Hebrew, Aramaic and Greek. Especially Greek, the language of the written New Testament (to us Christians, the words of Christ perfect and supersede those of the Hebrew Old Testament). So I studied the common Greek used in the source documents; discovered my interest and talent; and extended my studies to other and earlier forms of Greek, such as the language of Homer's Odyssey and the writers after him.

Then came my crisis. God pushed me away, or you can believe I ran if you wish, and my faith was lost. Theology changed from a fascinating exploration of an otherwise hidden, higher reality to a study without object: delving into the minutiae of myths in search of truths too large for them to hold.

I admit it is traumatic, to lose your faith. But if it broke a part of me, it also broke parts that deserved breaking. My drinking, which before had been limited to small quantities with good friends, became expanded in both volume, locale, and noisiness of the locales. I dabbled in the less harmful drugs, though I valued my mind too much to do more than experiment. Nor will it surprise you given those two admissions that my virginity did not last long.

If you think my sexual adventures added to my guilt, you are wrong. If anything they validated my loss of faith. Those delicious feelings I mentioned are but precursors to the act itself, which I am sure you are aware of yourself. What kind of God gives us a body capable of such glory then makes it a sin to enjoy it? I am a historian. I understand the origins of sexual morality, the disastrous effects of unwed pregnancy in the societies in which those mores arose. But even then the restrictions were excessive, as the experiences of less prudish cultures show us: in the same manner as making it a sin to eat pork, when merely cooking it properly to kill parasites achieves the same end. Moral sledgehammers to crush nuts. It makes even less sense to cling to such arbitrary rules in our modern age of disease control and contraception. Which no doubt accounts for how frequently they are broken even by those who most loudly proclaim their importance. And so I broke them, or more accurately ignored them with the contempt they deserve, gave as much pleasure as I received and nobody was harmed in the process. And what can possibly be wrong with that? If the amount of joy in the world increases, who dares call it sin, and on what grounds?

That was what became of my personal life, but what of my professional life? My love of ancient languages remained, and if I would not follow theology then I would pursue the objective reality behind it. But did I want the pure language to be found in museums and ancient texts, or a life more in the field, freeing the primary evidence from the Earth myself rather than interpreting things found by others? History, or archeology? The dust of museums, or the dust of the dry lands most conducive to the preservation of history; history that one day might be brought to light after how many millennia, to become a treasure in the present? I was torn. I loved languages, and could immerse myself in them. Yet I had always been active, enjoying many sports from swimming to tennis to martial arts, and perhaps the shade of Indiana Jones whispered to me. In any case I had time to decide: I would study both disciplines until my path revealed itself.

Then one day came the fifth signpost. I chanced upon an article about bitcoin, and I remembered my youthful dip in its waters. So I read it with amusement, wondering whether my future held a holiday, a car or a Big Mac. At first I did not understand what I was reading. It made no sense. But its examples gave the same answers as my own calculations. And then I knew that my forgotten acquaintance had been shockingly wrong. My two hundred had not become a thousand, or even ten thousand. It had become over twenty million dollars.

What do you do, if your life is transformed?

I could quit school and live a life of luxury and flitting from experience to experience for the rest of my days. But the thought did not interest me. I remembered that the original archaeologists were wealthy men, or men with wealthy patrons. The thought amused me. I could learn what I wished from my courses, and when I was ready I could fund my own research. And if I decided I didn't like it, I could do something else.

I cashed in half my bitcoins and became wealthy in the real world, not merely a virtual millionaire in the electronic one. I planted my money in soils that I thought would make it grow. I was not yet ready to plunge into a world of luxury. The idea seemed as yet unreal: too distant from my life up to that point, too unexpected in its genesis.

I tried to find the boy with fiery eyes who had given me this gift, to thank him for transforming my life, but he had vanished. Perhaps he was dead, and the thought brought sadness. I considered hiring private investigators. But if he had chosen to disappear, what right did I have to intrude into his privacy, and what poor payment for his generosity of spirit would that be? And if he were dead, did I really want to know? I am not one to avoid truths. But such a truth is too final, so final it opens no opportunities for action, only the gates to sorrow. I would rather hold to the hope that somewhere he lived, enjoying his own life to the full, and the best tribute I could give him would be to enjoy mine.

Thinking of him, it amused me to buy a car in homage to his prophecy. I would say I hope you will not judge me for my choice, except that if you are the kind who would condemn me for it you are not the kind whose opinions concern me. It was a Ferrari. I had always admired art that aspired; there was something about owning a Ferrari that touched the same chord in my soul. If it seems odd to you that a car can inspire a person's spirit, perhaps that is because you drive a Prius. I once read that the art you like is a reflection of your soul. It amuses me to imagine that the same is true of your car.

I also bought an apartment, high in a building next to a beach.

I mentioned art. I always liked beautiful art. Until now I had limited myself to prints; if feeling extravagant, a high quality giclée print rather than rolled up paper from an online store. Now one wall, opposite a full length mirror, holds a large original work, more vibrant in color and alive with texture than a print could be. It is a woman, naked in the moonlight, her arms reaching toward the full moon above. She is an image of sensuality and aspiration combined; and though the moon is far out of reach it seems that nothing is truly beyond her grasp, that even touching the moon lies within her power.

But other than those, and cultivating a rather more expensive taste in liquor, food and clothing, my lifestyle did not change much. I continued to study, though now I needed no degree as a passport to a career. My interest at the time was more literature and language than the march of history they sometimes recorded. So I followed my love of Greek writings from Homer to Plutarch; delved into the minds of their great thinkers from Aristotle to Archimedes.

And so I came to the sixth signpost of my life. It started with a doorbell. When I answered the door, a man stood there with an envelope and a package. He looked at me quizzically, as if I or his task mystified him. Then he shrugged and handed me the envelope, which below my name and address had written in large letters:

Open me first.

It was all very *Alice in Wonderland*, and I wondered what rabbit hole I was about to fall down.

Inside was a card on thick ivory paper, embossed in gold, with a faint gold bitcoin logo background. On the top it declared:

The Organizing Committee Invites

Angela Milton

To our Celebration Festivities

Beneath which was an address in Puerto Rico, a range of dates and a QR code.

Down the bottom in a flowing font was added:

Come and change the world

I think my own expression now matched the delivery man's, who then handed over the larger package. It too held my name and address, with another *Alice*-like message:

Wear me when you come

I gave the delivery man an incredulous look and generous tip for his trouble and he departed, whistling as cheerfully as tunelessly as he went.

I retreated inside. I opened the package and gasped. It was a dress. Full length and flowing, like a ball gown, made of a soft, rich fabric shimmering with a deep shade of reddish purple. I picked it up in wonder, as much at the unexpected nature of the anonymous gift as at its magnificence. I stripped to my underwear and put it on, twisting my body to and fro in front of the full length mirror in my hall. It hugged my skin like a caress. The material was somewhat thick, yet light and cool. Its color shimmered and changed, as if its deep hue seeped into the air around it. The fabric crossed my breasts and its folds fell down, leaving my arms bare except for loose diaphanous sleeves; it looked almost Grecian in style, as if I were Athena or Artemis come to life. What it was made of I could not guess: it was like no fabric I had ever seen or felt before.

I examined the effect critically. I do not think of myself as beautiful, but I have that rare and striking combination of auburn hair and blue eyes, yet with few freckles to mark my pale skin. The dress seemed to absorb the color of my hair, and my hair the color of the dress, as if each were made complete by the other. My eyes, I am told by those who know me well enough to experience my moods, vary in shade: from a hard grey blue when I am disinterested or contemptuous, to a sharp bright blue when I am nervous or excited. The latter are what looked back at me out of the mirror.

Whoever my mysterious benefactor was, he had provided only the dress. No shoes or jewelry accompanied it. What did that mean? Perhaps, like many men, he had no idea what should go with the dress: but unlike some men, he knew it. Perhaps he wished me the freedom to make my own choices. Or perhaps it was a test. I decided I owed the giver of such a gift a kind interpretation, so chose freedom.

I wondered why he (if it were indeed a man) had sent me his invitation and gift, and at the incongruity between the impersonal formality of the former and the very personal nature of the latter. I considered whether I should accept either.

I knew I would.

And so here I am, standing alone in this strange party. When I arrived at the airport I was greeted by a chauffeur bearing my name, and he whisked me and my luggage to this old monastery; where we were passed over to a crisply dressed, polite young man who continued the whisking to my room. There I dressed; now I have arrived. I wonder what the final destination of the signposts will truly be.

I wear his dress, and I have matched it with golden sandals on my feet, an armlet of real gold on my arm, and a headband shot through with braided gold and silver thread around my hair. The rest of my hair coils down the side of my head. A large and perfect amethyst hangs on a gold chain around my neck, condensing the color of my dress into its own clearer and deeper purple, radiating its light into the sparkle of the smaller diamonds that surround it. I wear earrings of short diamond chains ending in teardrops of blue topaz, their color matching my eyes.

Do you think I do this to flaunt my wealth? I have no desire for such pettiness, and were I so foolish, it is clear that I would have achieved only shame not conceit: for many here are far wealthier than

I am. But the dress demands it; and I cannot wear it if I do not match its beauty, nor accept my benefactor's gift without honoring him by doing so.

I expect to be greeted by him with smiles and explanations. But as I make my way through the people here, I receive nothing beyond the standard greetings of strangers. Those who look at me do so as if looking for a friend but not finding her; or with the curiosity occasioned by a novel sight. Some give me more searching glances, drawn to the beauty of my gown or, from the glint in their eyes, by anticipation of the beauty they imagine lies beneath it. But no eyes display the light of recognition.

It is a strange party, awash with sashimi and tequila and not much else. There are worse problems to cope with. I have to admit the sashimi is divine and the tequila burning, and I begin to lose myself in the celebration.

Do not think I was incurious. Despite the minimalist invitation it did not take too much research to find out the nature of the party. It is a celebration of bitcoin millionaires. Some, I believe, are even billionaires. I wonder how many of them are, like me, accidental millionaires. It does not seem to matter. Accidental or not, I am one of them. Perhaps nobody has greeted me because many such invitations were sent, by some secretary working off a list, and there is nothing special about me after all. But then I wonder about my dress. While many here are dressed as if they wish to hide their wealth—or perhaps they simply do not care about what covers their skin—still there are many expensive and even spectacular clothes on display here, on women and men alike. Though none seem made of the same strange fabric that forms mine.

The party is not a mere celebration of good fortune. What little information was publicly available, and the conversations I overhear, agree that these people want to change the world. They seem to think they can succeed. Perhaps that is just the hubris of those who have fallen by luck into a fortune, and think it is proof of a personal brilliance that nothing can resist. I wonder how long their enthusiasm will survive the end of this party; how long before some or most of the brilliantly alive people here dissolve into hedonism or self-destruction or both. Time, I suppose, will tell, as it tells all.

But for now their enthusiasm and optimism are infectious, and I eat their sashimi, drink their tequila, laugh at their jokes, and am enthralled at their vision of a future in which this mysterious blockchain, on which bitcoin is built, is not just a means to unexpected wealth but the foundation of a new era. I hear of the promise of all people great and small in control of their own destiny; of dignity and identity for the dispossessed; of aid freely given and received and repaid without waste or fraud or corruption; of incorruptible records to preserve and trace everything from money to diamonds to ideas.

I stand with a group of people discussing these thoughts, new possibilities sparking off each other like a critical mass generating a chain reaction. They begin to speak of cities on the ocean, communities of equals beyond the reach of politicians who would rule and bureaucrats who would control just because they can. Then I hear a voice from beyond the group, behind me.

"Do you know what we are?" he asks. Heads turn respectfully, and I realize that unlike me, the speaker is well known among these people. I suspect that means his wealth vastly exceeds mine. I turn to see him, and after a moment recognize my friend from years ago, the boy who made me rich, now a man who exudes quiet power. The man, no doubt, who invited me here. The thought had simmered in my mind, but I had refused to accept it, thinking he must have forgotten me. Or in shame that I had never sought him out more persistently, a shame made worse if it was he who had sought me out. Perhaps he agreed with my guilt, and my spurning of him is why he chose to ignore me, and address the group rather than me personally.

"We are the New Phoenicians," he replies to his own question, looking directly into my eyes, and I realize that it is to me he speaks after all. The others are just incidental actors on a stage of his setting.

"What do you mean?" I ask. I know of the Phoenicians, of course, for their civilization lasted thousands of years and spread throughout the lands around the Mediterranean Sea, with an influence felt even today. But they are neither my specialty nor my greatest interest, and my knowledge of them is more in their relationships with the Greeks and Romans than with the details of their civilization itself.

"The Phoenicians had the first intercontinental empire. Long before Alexander, before Rome, their cities and outposts spread around the Mediterranean, from Lebanon to Europe and across the top of Africa to Spain and the islands in between; they traded beyond the Straits of Gibraltar as far as England. But do you know what was most peculiar about their empire?"

A few murmur in response, but I do not hear their answers.

"They were not an empire of conquest, but of trade," he continues. "Alexander conquered the world, or as much of it as he could reach. The other empires before and after were won by armies too: defeating city after city, people after people, so that they could be ruled and tribute paid to their overlords. But the Phoenicians were traders. Their wealth came from trade. Their influence came from trade.

"Did you know they were the first significant culture to use an alphabet? And they spread its influence wherever they went. Their alphabet was the ancestor of the Hebrew alphabet, the Greek alphabet: and through it the Roman alphabet and most alphabets around the entire world."

"Why did you say we are the new Phoenicians?" I ask.

"Because like them, our empire will cross borders and span the world: not through conquest or government force, but through trade of values. Like them, our influence will come from trade and wealth. Like them, our currency is knowledge and worth.

"Do you know where their name comes from?" he adds. "Phoenicians?"

My brain seems frozen: by tequila or too many fresh ideas, I cannot tell. I know I know this, but it is temporarily beyond my power to answer, beyond the one soft word: "Purple."

"Yes," he says. "It is from the Greek for purple. Much of their original wealth came from a purple dye they learned how to purify from murex sea snails. It was fabulously expensive, not only because it took thousands of snails to make an ounce, but because its beautiful color actually intensified in sunlight. Instead of fading away, it got richer. If anyone wonders what color it was: well, there it is," he points. At me. At my dress. "The color varied with the quality, but that reddish purple is within the range of the best of them, as far as anyone can tell today."

I look down at my dress, and finally understand. I look back up at him, my mouth an 'O', my tongue frozen. I think the crowd is making noises of appreciation, but it washes over me unheard.

I do not know how long this timeless moment lasts. It is broken by a question from the crowd. "So what happened to them?"

"It seems the fate of empires to decline, no matter how powerful. In their case, they lost their homeland to the Persians but rose again elsewhere as the great city of Carthage. But then they became an enemy of Rome. Three times they fought Rome, in the famous Punic Wars. Three times they lost, and then Carthage was destroyed. The Phoenicians still existed, but that was the end of their power."

"That was Hannibal, right?" a voice interjects. "Him and the elephants, crossing the Alps."

I know this. While not an expert, I know the basic history of the Phoenicians. I even knew about the purple, though not its exact shade or its link to my dress. But I keep silent. This is his tale to tell, not mine.

"Yes. The first Punic War was fought over a disagreement in Sicily, with the two powers supporting different cities. A generation later, war brewed again and Hannibal decided to take the battle to them. He thought if he was successful on Italian soil, that Rome's allies would desert her and that Rome would negotiate. He underestimated the allies' fear or love of Rome, and Roman intransigence and persistence. He was one of the greatest generals who ever lived, but despite some spectacular victories he could never bring the battle to Rome itself. So as the years dragged on, final victory slipped from his grasp. At the end, a Roman general who was his equal, Scipio, took sail to threaten Carthage itself, and Hannibal was forced to leave Italy to defend it. There Scipio beat him, and that was the end of the second Punic War and a further blow to Carthaginian power and influence.

"Another fifty years went by, until Rome was no longer content to have its rival live. So they started the third Punic War. This time it was the Romans attacking Carthage. It didn't take long. After only three years of siege they took the city, killed or enslaved its inhabitants, and utterly destroyed Carthage."

He seems to have forgotten me, and looks around at his audience. "Can you envisage how the world might have been different if Hannibal had won? Imagine it: if instead of militaristic Rome expanding its empire across Europe and the Middle East, a different empire, one that had armies but was still fundamentally based on trade, had grown in its place? Some people think that if Hannibal had marched on Rome straight after his great victories, he might have pulled it off. Hannibal himself regretted not doing so, later in life. But most historians say he could never have won. That the Romans were too committed to their own city and sovereignty. That Hannibal was never going to get enough support from home to become powerful enough to take Rome. That without siege engines, the attempt would have been hopeless. But perhaps... perhaps... what if he had? Much of the world was shaped by the Romans, a race who ruled by iron and tribute. Their influence so great that even in modern times our rulers have still named themselves after Caesar, from the Czars to the Kaisers."

He pauses, looking around at his audience, before adding:

"What if there had been no Caesars?"

The listeners are silent for a while, pondering his words. Then conversations begin to break out, and I hear excited comments on the past and the possible future. Whether the people here would truly become the nucleus of a new Phoenicia. I hear one group return to the idea they had started on earlier, the crazy idea that had been literally floated recently: new cities, new countries, built on the ocean itself. Modern technology could do it. All it would take is money and will. I feel a thrill in my own bones, at the thought that while the old Phoenicia and all its possibilities had been lost, perhaps I am witnessing the birth of the new.

My friend has not forgotten or spurned me after all, and somehow I find myself drawn away from the crowd. He guides me to a small, quiet balcony, festooned with vines sporting large, pale yellow flowers that seem to glow in the moonlight. A couple of people are standing here, leaning against the railing, smoking something that might or might not be tobacco, but at a subtle motion of his head they smile and leave us in privacy. The monastery is built on the side of a hill and overlooks the coast, and I look out at the gently washing waves in the distance, and at a big hawk moth humming its way around the fragrant flowers.

I feel unaccountably nervous for a multimillionaire; in my hand is a tequila shot I had unconsciously lifted from a tray on my way here, and it burns its way down my throat as I toss it down in a single gulp. I cannot look at my friend. I do not know why.

For the first time, he addresses me personally.

"Hello, Angela."

The simple normalcy of it in the face of the extravagance of the invitation, the dress and the party breaks my resistance, and I laugh and face him at last. "Hello, Ricky."

Thus I meet simplicity with simplicity. Truly, I am amazing. Awesome times five, as I used to say to my dad.

When I say no more, he smiles and waves his hand at the moth still poking its nose into the flowers. It darts from one to the other, then hovers in place, its long proboscis probing the flower's feminine depths as a faint hum emanates from its blurring wings. I wonder if the sexual connotation is what he wishes to draw my attention to, or whether that is birthed from my own mind. I get my answer when he speaks.

"It is amazing, isn't it? This moth has a brain the size of a pinhead, yet it does feats of flying that a supercomputer would have trouble matching in real time. I wonder what we will be capable of, when our computers have the same density and efficiency of processing power?"

I laugh, in simple delight at the unexpectedness of his observation, in amusement at the contrast to my own less elevated observations. I suspect I have had too much tequila.

But whatever it is, we are friends again, if ever we were not, and my tongue decides it is capable of complex speech after all.

"I have so much to thank you for, Ricky, I just don't know where to start."

He laughs. "It cost me nothing. It didn't even cost me that hundred dollars I offered you. Advice to a friend isn't a cost, Angela. Don't you see? It enriches the giver as much as the recipient. I wouldn't have given you the advice if I didn't like you. I am glad you took my advice. I am happy that you are happy."

"Were we friends, Ricky?" I ask softly. I did not lie earlier. I did consider him a friend, albeit a peripheral one. But here is a man who transformed my life, and then tracked me down to give me another amazing experience. A man whom I liked, in passing; but did not like enough to seek him out, then or now. I owe him at least the honesty of my question.

He smiles, but I think I see some sadness in his eyes. "We were friends, Angela. I... I never told you how I felt about you. I think you knew, even if I wasn't what you were looking for. But that's OK. Nobody owns another person, and we all have to make our own choices and live with them. But if I liked... loved... you more than you did me, well, I'm far from the only person ever in that position. If we don't seek values, then we might as well be dead. But the whole reason we need to seek values is because they aren't guaranteed. Don't worry, Angela. We were friends then and we are friends now, whatever the future holds. Even if we never see each other again, we have had what we have had."

There is something in the tone of his ending; an undercurrent of danger or despair, and I wonder what it means. "What do you mean?" I ask. Truly, I am amazing, as I have noted before.

There is something in the way he pauses before answering, which makes me feel his reply is only part of the truth.

"Who can predict the future? You've seen the people tonight. High on their success; full of hope for a bright future. But how many of them will crash and burn? How many will just drift into a life without fire or purpose?

"Which of those fates will be worse?"

His words echo my own earlier thoughts, and I give him a searching glance. "And what fate do you see for me?" I ask.

"You will choose your own fate. We all do. Even if it chooses us because we allow ourselves to drift on the currents of time, it is we who chose to drift. I don't mean that if we fail it is our fault. But it is our fault if we fail to try."

There is something strange about his words, and I feel unaccountably afraid to pursue them further. He seems to feel the same tension, and changes the topic.

"You look beautiful in that dress. You have chosen the accessories perfectly. You look like a goddess."

I surprise myself by blushing. My social skills and sophistication tonight are exemplary.

"The dress is beautiful, Ricky. I've never seen a material like it. What is it made of?"

"It is an experimental material being developed by a startup I've invested in. Carbon nanotubes and graphene combined with Kevlar. The way they are made is why the fabric shimmers. It is also temperature adaptive: the pores open more in the warmth. So while it isn't perfect, it is warmer when you are cold, and cooler when you are hot."

"Kevlar? So I'm wearing a bullet-proof vest as well?"

He laughs. "Actually, you aren't far wrong. Carbon nanotubes are even stronger than Kevlar. So if you wrapped yourself in it fairly tightly, it would act like a bulletproof vest. I don't think it would stop a magnum, or even a smaller bullet fired point blank, but a smaller caliber fired from a distance… perhaps it could save your life."

I laugh with delight. I don't know what else to do. It is all so wonderfully ludicrous. So is the look on his face, which looks incongruously serious as he speaks of dangers unlikely to ever threaten me.

His eyes light up as if hit with a sudden idea. "There is something I want to show you. It is a bit of a walk from here, but it's worth it."

"What is it?"

"Something… magical."

A feeling of caution tells me no, but the feeling is outvoted by something akin to recklessness. The recklessness ups the ante by taking his hand in mine as I reply simply, "Sure."

And so we leave the monastery and walk along a path up the hill, the sandy gravel of the path crunching lightly beneath our feet and soft leaves gently stroking us as we pass, as if the forest is welcoming us into its domain. We come to the entrance of a cave lightly screened by flowering vines, these too graced with an attendant moth. Ricky parts the vines and leads me inside into an entrance soft with a carpet of leaves deposited by the wind. We do not need to go far before it is too dark to see further, and we stop; the only sounds are our breathing and the gentle sound of a small stream burbling somewhere in the darkness.

"Close your eyes and count to sixty, then open them again."

When I open my eyes, the world is like black velvet studded with thousands of phosphorescent stars. With no depth cues except their variable glow, it is as if they extend into infinity.

"Glow worms," he explains.

"Wow," I breathe in response. "Ricky! It's beautiful!"

We say nothing more, both lost in this sight, with nothing visible but blackness and stars, as if we are suspended in a place out of time and space.

At last we return to the world.

In the distance, lightning flashes from dark clouds, and some long seconds later a long peal of thunder rolls through the sky. I feel something strange in the air, like a breath drawn; the hairs on my arms lift in answer to it. The moth, perhaps sensing the same thing and its pinhead mind deducing a need for shelter, hovers once then darts away into the night.

"A storm is coming," Ricky says. As he says it I feel his arm around my waist. He is looking away towards the storm and I do not think he even knows he did it; it seems more like an instinctive gesture of protection.

I look at him and something stirs within me. "Ricky, I'm really tired, can you walk me back to my room?" I intend to ask, but I find I am unable to utter the protective lie.

"Ricky, can you walk me back to my room?"

He gives me a look of surprise, both at my words and at the fact that he holds me. This time deliberately, he puts his arm through mine like a couple promenading; but as we start to walk he looks again at the coming storm.

"I don't think I can walk you to your room."

"Why not?"

"We need to run."

We run along the path, giggling like a pair of teenagers as we race the storm clouds. My maturity tonight is truly astounding. But since in some highly relevant ways I feel I wasted my teenage years, I forgive myself the lapse.

We reach shelter just as the first drops of rain start hitting us, and we stop to catch our breath. Then we rediscover our dignity and resume a more stately walk to my room.

I find myself outside my room. The world now seems to be spinning around me as if the full force of all that tequila has finally arrived, and I find myself wondering how I came to be here. I unlock the door and turn to face him, but do not know what to say.

"Well," he says.

"Well," I reply in my usual witty fashion.

Oh for God's sake, I say to myself. With one hand I reach behind myself to open the door, and after kicking it open I take his hand and drag him inside. Perhaps 'drag' is a misnomer, for I do not encounter much resistance.

He holds me, searching my face with eyes that hold a fierce hunger, as if seeing an oasis long imagined but never reached. But he holds back, as if now he has reached its shore he is afraid to drink from it, in case it vanishes again into a mirage.

"You... you have drunk a lot, Angela. I don't want to... you know... do anything you'll regret."

Oh for heaven's sake, can't a man and woman get it on any more without signed declarations?

"Ricky... shut up. Just. Shut. Up. I might be tipsy but I'm not paralytic."

Part of me wonders if I deceive myself, for truth be told, my world appears to be swaying around its edges. But I cannot hold to the thought, which itself wavers and is gone, leaving nothing but a burning desire.

I want to shut him up by a more direct method, but feel a sudden surge of cruelty in response to his hesitation. So I bend away from him, a slight smile on my lips, and look up into his eyes, daring him to act. Promising him that he will not achieve his desire if he fails to act; praying that he will not fail.

Thankfully he takes the hint. He enfolds me in his arms, and his lips meet mine.

More than his lips, I notice. This dress might be bulletproof, but it does nothing to stop the pressure of his growing desire, if you know what I mean. I sigh, as I decide to investigate his tongue with mine. My dress seems to dissolve off my shoulders and fall to the ground, and my underwear follows, while I frantically do the same to him.

I laugh at my earlier self, that pure innocent who was afraid to take a few notes of cash for fear it would lead her into irredeemable sin. I laugh because I refused the money yet here we are anyway: if that was truly his goal back then, this must qualify as the longest range seduction in history. Do not misunderstand. I am not offering any criticism, except perhaps of the foolish virgin I once was, who valued an illusory purity over a guiltless ecstasy.

I don't know whether he pushes me to my bed or I drag him there, but now here we are, entwined in passion. This isn't the best sex I have ever had, but I'm not complaining; I don't notice him complaining either. Or perhaps I am wrong. Not about complaining, but about the sex, as the pleasure thrusts and rolls and grows. The distant storm is now fully upon us, and I hear its downpour drumming on the outside, punctuated by the flash and thunder of lightning. I laugh, as it seems as if we and the storm are in another race, this time to see which of us will reach our climax first.

I have definitely had too much tequila to drink and too many ideas to think. The groaning of the bed sounds like the creaking of the timbers of a ship, and as I feel the world rolling around me, I imagine I am on such a ship, rocking and rolling with the waves as it carries a cargo of purple and silver and gold. I feel this man possessing me, and for a moment I cannot tell whether he is Hannibal the man who lost Old Phoenicia, or a man of another age who dreams of giving birth to the New. Then the two worlds fuse into one, and I know nothing but the pleasure of our union. I see his dark eyes staring into mine with desire and joy, then as I feel him come inside me and I gasp in my own answering orgasm, the lightning crashes outside our sanctuary. Then it is as if time stops for long moments: I see silver flame reflected in his burning black eyes, before those eyes expand to fill a world that suddenly goes dark.

Chapter 2: The City

L a petite mort.

I have heard of it, but it has never happened to me before: the 'little death' some women experience after orgasm. But that must have been what I experienced, given the nature of my last memory still etched in my brain and my flesh.

I sigh, wondering if it has been minutes or hours since that moment. Then I notice I feel a little cold, and I open my eyes in surprise.

They open to a strange place. At first I do not know it is strange. Perhaps the noises are unexpected: but I realize I do not know what I expect. Dawn is breaking, its soft light suffusing the sky.

Now that is strange.

Why is it strange? I must still be drunk, for I feel it is strange without knowing why. I expect a headache, but find my head is clear of pain, if not yet clear in perception. I am naked, and this reminds me again of last night. You will be unsurprised to know that the memory is pleasant. So pleasant that my body insists on reminding me again, and suggests that a further performance, perhaps on the same theme but with variations, like a sparkling Bach arrangement, could be to our mutual advantage.

Things are coming together now.

Signposts again, pointing the way to the truth.

Signpost one. Why can I see the sky through a large rectangular hole in the wall, which lets in not just the sight of the sky but a gentle breeze? There should be a window with pleasant curtains, immune to wind and rain, not a rough wall with a big hole in it.

Signpost two. Why do I hear animal noises through that hole?

Signpost three. I know I am naked because a thin, rough blanket is rubbing against my otherwise nicely tender nipples and scratching my skin.

Signpost four. A repeat of the more vigorously happy assault on those nipples seems unlikely, for when I reach out my arms I find I am alone.

On the floor.

On a thin layer of straw.

In a room that smells like donkeys or horses or something. Covered in the tattiest blanket I've ever seen, which looks and smells like something worn by one of the donkeys until even the donkey threw it away in disgust.

I emit a startled squeak, the equal of last night's sublime eloquence, and sit up in fright.

What the hell?

Is someone playing a weird joke on me? Then a sick feeling hits me, and it is not a hangover. Perhaps it was all an act. Oh, I am quite sure Ricky was happy to have me. He certainly got his money's worth last night. Well, the hundred dollars not the twenty million, anyway: I am not that conceited about my sensual powers. But maybe that's all he wanted; or despite his words, my cavalier attitude toward him those years ago led to resentment, and resentment brewed into a baroque plan of vengeance. I cringe at the things I said; my talk of friendship; my imaginings about the past. What an idiot.

So he drugged me, slept with me, then carted me away from my luxury apartment and dumped me down at the wharves or some other pesthole in the poor part of town. *Christ!* He's probably back at the bar right now, laughing with his real friends about his most excellent practical-joke-with-benefits. I want to sue the bastard, though I don't know how I could prove anything. He probably has twenty witnesses to testify that I got plastered and wandered off on my own to see the sights, over his gallant protestations.

Then the implications of the obvious finally hit me.

Naked.

Oh crap, I'm still naked. In a lousy part of town with no money, no sense and no idea. *Idiot!* I'm sure that will make the joke even funnier. To them. I blush deep red at the mere thought of my return to the monastery like some kind of Lady Godiva cosplay. Minus cos.

But when I look around I see my clothes in an untidy pile near my feet, including my dress and even my jewelry. This puzzles me. It seems out of character for my new, more realistically cynical model of Ricky and his motives. Why would he dump me here but leave me my clothes? Even if he had sufficient shred of decency left to not want to see me running through the streets like a demented streaker, I could have managed with this crappy blanket. Not well, and not without an embarrassing show for the locals to laugh about, but well enough.

I pride myself on my strength. But I cannot help it. I cry, sobbing into my hands, desolate and alone. I cry for five minutes, or maybe it was less than one, until finally I wipe my eyes on the back of my hand and pull myself together and to my feet.

Quickly, I dress. The last thing I want added to my shame is for some wide-eyed yokel to wander in and catch me naked. I hesitate at my jewelry, then savagely put it back on. If I'm wearing the dress, I'm wearing the rest: let him laugh, let his friends point, but I will walk back with my head held high. Screw the lot of them.

I briefly wonder if this will make me a target of violence but I discard the thought. I cling to the theory that while he wishes me to suffer he does not wish me to be harmed. Else why would he have left the clothes at all? This part of the city, though obviously seedy and poor, must be reasonably safe. And if I do have to call for help, I hope a higher class appearance will make help more likely to arrive.

There is no door, just another hole, and I wander out into the street. There is some kind of port nearby, a street or so away from where I am. I smell the sea air on a gentle breeze from the ocean, ridden by scores of gulls crying to each other in their ageless call. I can see some boats on the harbor, but they are peculiar vessels. They all appear to be decrepit sailing vessels: not a gleaming motor launch or container ship among them, and I wonder what the hell kind of harbor this is. Some theme village perhaps? *Come, immerse yourself in the colorful past of this picturesque port town! Infested with merchants eager to replace your money with gaudy trash!*

Terrific. Just terrific.

It is early but there are a few people around, most pushing squeaking trolleys full of mysterious goods. They are mainly dressed in rather grubby tunics, from which nut-brown knobby legs descend into rough sandals. I wonder what movie set they all escaped from.

Then I have a suspicious thought. That bastard is a billionaire.

Maybe movie set is what it is. Dump the bitch into it, sprinkle it with unsavory actors, and put the whole embarrassing mess up on YouTube. What a laugh. *Angela's Excellent Adventures in Blunderland.*

I walk up to a wall and pound it with my fist. Feels solid enough. I walk around a few frontages. They all have backages. I take a closer look at the inhabitants. I catch a few sly looks that quickly slide off to examine interesting insects or stones elsewhere. They all avoid me.

"Hello?" I say. "Can anyone help me?"

They all either ignore me or look at me with puzzled frowns then ignore me. If they are actors I would expect something more creative. I recall that Spanish is most widely spoken here, and while I am hardly an expert I know enough to get by on.

Alas, "¿Hola? ¿Alguien puede ayudarme?" doesn't do any better.

But at least my attempts have prompted some of them to start their own conversations and I listen in, trying to identify the language. Mystifying. It is a language I don't recall hearing; the nearest I can think of is a faint resemblance to Hebrew.

One of them decides to talk at me, waving his arms around for emphasis, but I have no more idea what he is saying than he does me. Soon enough he frowns and gives up, resuming muttering to his colleagues.

I wander down the street; down a few others. Some people shout at me or point at me; most ignore me; they all seem to speak the same tongue.

What the hell is this place? Some Jewish version of an Amish colony?

Nobody has made a hostile move or spoken to me in a tone I would interpret as hostile. But as I continue my mystified wandering, I begin to notice the occasional watcher in the shadows or a group muttering in a doorway while casting suspicious glances in my direction, and I start to feel nervous. I am not afraid yet. I might be an academic with a fondness for history, but I retain the athleticism of my youth, or at least some of it. I was a very good swimmer, doing well in competitions though never having enough interest or dedication to aim for world class. Then I put those muscles to different use when I became keen on martial arts for several years. I became quite good at unarmed combat, including against armed opponents. Then other interests took over and my practice sessions declined, usually limited to times when things were going wrong and I needed something to hit for a while. But still I know my reflexes live on, slightly rusty but working, and looking at these people I feel I could handle any one or two of them. But if they ganged up on me...

Giving such thoughts a foothold is a mistake. My anger that my being here is some kind of trick starts dying, morphing into the cold fear of an unprotected woman flaunting jewelry in a slum. If this is a trick, it is both too extended and too subtle next to the crudity of what went before. The air smells too strange and the people act weirdly normal, as if it is I who am the anomaly; and none of it makes any sense. I feel the tears beginning to prick my eyes again.

Laugh away, you little bastard, I think, the only thing greater than my fury at the idea of him watching and laughing being my fear that nobody is watching me at all. It is a feeble attempt to assert anger over fear that quickly fails, and I can feel the panic beginning to grow.

Then with a sudden wrench my perspective switches. Until now I have seen this place, these people, as strangers in my world. But now I feel as if it is I who am the stranger in theirs. I look again at the people, the buildings, and everything else, and it is as if I have awoken in the distant past. The thought is insanity, but now I have let it in I cannot shake it, and every open glance and closed door takes on a patina of menace. The panic sees its chance and grabs it.

Then a man appears around the corner in front of me. He is dressed much better than the rough workers I have seen so far, and he holds himself like a man used to getting his own way. When he sees me he stops still, staring, apparently as startled to see me as I am to see him. I stare back and pray to the God I no longer believe in that I have finally found a man who might bring some answers.

Chapter 3: The Native

I have not been back in the chief city of my people for long and am not sure how long I shall remain. I have been sent here by my brother to strengthen some alliances, flatter some enemies, and perhaps find men strong of arm and clear of mind to add to our growing power abroad.

I shake my head at the thought of some of my people, wondering why it can take argument and browbeating to convince them of the obvious; wondering why we are riven with rivalries and pettiness. Do they not see that our very survival is at stake? Do they not see the danger, not yet broken out, but lying in wait? Yet all they care about are their petty ambitions and holding on to their petty corruptions. So many fools.

My angry thoughts are wiped clean by a most unexpected sight. As I reach the next street I am greeted by a vision. For a moment I am struck dumb, for she is like no woman I have ever seen. She must be fabulously wealthy, for she wears a long dress of the richest purple, adorned with gold and jewels. And such workmanship! What world made those gems, cut with exquisitely symmetric perfection? What world made that dress, with sleeves so fine it seems her arms are clothed with mist? The being within matches her attire in strangeness. She has hair the color of dark fire to match the purple and eyes to match the sky, and for a moment I imagine she must be a goddess descended to Earth. I remember the tales from long ago, when the gods visited men, for good or ill.

I chide myself for my childish thoughts. It is a fool who fails to give the gods honor, but if once they ever walked among men those days are long gone. And how could she be a goddess? When I can see past her magnificence I see her eyes are wide with fear and wet with tears.

Then who is she, and where did she come from? Why is she here in this part of the city? It makes no sense.

I have heard of people with hair like hers among the northern barbarians. But no barbarian ever looked like her: if they did, truly it would be we who are the barbarians. She cannot be a slave: no master would bestow such finery on one such as that. Her robe has a Grecian look about it. Perhaps if she is not a goddess she is the priestess of some cult? But if she is not a slave, and has the high station she must, why is she here alone with no attendants? If she is rich enough for her raiment, why is she stumbling around on foot? Why does she appear so lost and afraid? I wonder whether she has been injured, perhaps fallen from a horse, or escaped from villains who waylaid her? The realization jolts me out of my shock.

I ask her if she is hurt or needs help, but she looks at me as if my words have no more meaning than the wind. Then she utters something in a strange tongue. I have encountered many peoples in my travels, but this is not a tongue I recognize. Our encounter gets stranger and stranger. Could she be some foreign princess? The victim of shipwreck or pirates, washed ashore or escaped?

All educated men know Greek, and if she is princess or priestess, perhaps so does she. I repeat my question in Greek, and am rewarded by a glimmer of recognition in her eyes and a hopefully searching glance. I repeat it again, speaking slowly and clearly.

"You... you are speaking Old Greek?" she asks. Her accent is awful and I must have misunderstood, for there is nothing old about my Greek. But I understand well enough, I think.

"Yes, my Lady. I am speaking Greek. Are you in trouble?"

She sighs, as if she has been drowning and her flailing arms have touched a raft. "I... where am I, noble sir?"

I look around, puzzled. "You are on the street of the flour merchants. You have come from the direction of the old animal pens near the wharf."

My answer seems to confuse her the more. "No! I mean, *where* am I? *What city?*" she asks, her voice rising toward hysteria.

"Why, Carthago of course. Where else?"

"Car... Carthago? *The* Carthago?" Strangely, her eyes have grown wide with terror, as if the great city of my homeland harbors not civilization but horror.

Her strangeness amuses me. "The greatest city of the Canaani, yes."

Then her eyes roll up and her legs fold beneath her. Out of reflex, I reach forward and catch her before she collapses onto the stones of the street.

I should have let her fall. Now that I have caught her I have made her my problem. For a moment I hold her up by her armpits, then I scoop my arms under her legs and back and lift her against my chest, wondering what I should do with her. Her problems are not my concern; perhaps she is not even innocent, and I put myself and more importantly my mission at risk by giving her aid. Or perhaps she is innocent, but her enemies are powerful, and the danger the same.

I should abandon her here, leaving her fate in the hands of the gods not mine. But looking at her, I know I cannot. None have dared attack her yet, showing wise prudence at the wrath of men or gods if one so exquisite were harmed. But looking at her jewels, I know that sooner rather than later their temptation will overcome caution. Cowardice is not in my nature, while hospitality to strangers is. She is a stranger, lost and frightened, who has asked me for help. How can I refuse it, and live with honor? I recall again the tales of long ago, of gods visiting men in disguise, seeking hospitality and, receiving it, granting rewards; or being spurned, calling down punishment. I have enough problems with men without risking the enmity of gods. I adjust her limp form into an easier position and carry her home, ignoring the inquisitive glances of those staring at what even I admit must be a most curious sight.

CHAPTER 4: ANGELA

I drift toward consciousness but refuse to open my eyes.
It must have been a nightmare, that strange vision of wandering the streets of ancient Carthage, a city dead for millennia. When I open my eyes, I will see my room in the monastery; perhaps find a man beside me whom I cursed in my dream so unfairly. I know this. Yet I feel strangely reluctant to prove it.

I smile at my stupidity and decide that the tequila they served here must have been infused with peyote, to produce such lucid yet bizarre dreams. *Of course it was a dream.* I sigh happily, and open my eyes.

I close my eyes. *No. No. No.*

I open my eyes and look around. I am in a better place than the one I woke up in last time, but it is still not the room I went to bed in. I am lying on a thin mattress, and there are murals painted on the walls, not especially ugly but nor do they display exceptional skill. But the air feels and smells the same, and the sounds of life from outside share the same unfamiliar character as before.

I notice I am naked. Again. Why must I lose my clothes every time the world goes dark on me? The realization of my nakedness produces a jolt of fear when I remember the strange man I met just before my latest inability to cope. But I feel no pain and can detect no signs of violation on my body, so at least I am spared that much. Looking around further, I see my clothes on a small table, this time neatly folded rather than just thrown on the floor. Next to them are what look like simpler clothes, perhaps some kind of off-white wool. I get up and feel them. A shift with a tunic, similar to what I saw the female natives—

for that is how I now think of them—wearing. I think these will do, and be less dramatic and brazen than my own clothes, so quickly I put them on.

I realize I need to find a toilet, and I wonder how I am to achieve this feat. A woman with an air of 'servant' walks past my door and seeing me up and about stops and looks at me, though whether out of curiosity or the habit of waiting for orders I do not know. I manage to make my need understood, and she nods, speaks some gibberish and gestures for me to follow her.

She guides me to a room and points inside, before departing on her original errand. I look inside, and see a long plank with six holes cut in it; one of them already occupied.

Oh dear Lord. You must be kidding me.

I observe the spectacle, aghast. It appears these people have rather different attitudes to modesty and privacy than I am used to. But I cannot think of any alternatives that aren't even worse than this one. Logic comes to my rescue, or as close as possible to rescue under the circumstances. If I am dreaming, it doesn't matter. And if I am not dreaming, I'm damn well going to have to get used to it. So I go in and sit as far away from the incumbent as I can. At least she is a woman. She glances at me curiously, but as at a stranger not at strange or offensive behavior, then resumes the privacy of her own thoughts, which is all the privacy either of us is going to get.

Despite my embarrassment, I decide I am glad this other woman is here. It allows me to surreptitiously observe the customs she follows. Soon enough she is done and gone, and I finish up as well. I will spare you the details: it's not as if you're likely to ever find yourself in my predicament, and I've had enough humiliation for one day.

The latrine is somewhat smelly but not unbearable; they must keep it clean, and there are bunches of fragrant dried herbs around. But I wouldn't say the hygiene here is stellar. As I leave I look back and give the room and its holey plank a sour glance. I fear this place is going to feature in my future rather more than I would like, until my body and the local army of microbes finally reach an uneasy détente.

The servant has returned and is waiting for me in the corridor. She again indicates I should follow her, and she leads me a short distance until we come upon my rescuer, sitting at a table watching me. He gestures for me to sit, and points at some plates of food and what looks like watered down wine.

I sit and offer him a smile. "I haven't thanked you, noble sir. So thank you, for helping me."

He does not smile, just watches me with his dark eyes, alive with a penetrating intelligence.

"You did not leave me much choice. I could not leave you lying in the street. Now tell me who you are, what you are and where you came from."

Despite his abrupt words, his tone is cool but not hostile. He seems to be more curious than anything else, yet alert to danger. I cannot blame him for that under the circumstances.

He looks at my clothes as if my choice means something to him, and I quail under his inspection, feeling like a chess novice whose efforts are being studied by a grandmaster who always sees five moves ahead. This is a man used to making decisions and having the power to carry them out. Despite what he has done for me and his neutral manner, I am sure my life depends on my answers. But what answers can I give? I have found that the truth is usually the best policy. But in this case the truth, if I even know what that is, would be the fastest route to my destruction.

"My name is Angela," I tell him. "As for the rest... noble sir, I cannot tell you. I did not know I was in Carthage and I do not know how I came to be here. As for where I am from, if I told you, you would think me mad. Can you accept that I am a stranger here, who knows little and means nobody any harm, least of all a man who rescued me?"

"Angela..." he replies, with a strange emphasis. "Indeed? How curious."

I am not sure what is so curious about it, but I need to break his stare, and realize I have my own questions.

"I apologize, sir. But I cannot say how I came to be here, for I do not know myself. But I have given you my name, and it is true. May I ask yours?"

"I am Hannibal, son of Hamilcar the Lightning."

I stare at him, feeling the world swaying around me again, afraid I will faint or failing that, throw up. "Of course you are," I whisper. "Who else would you be?" I can say no more, and continue to stare at him, the only stable point in the spinning reality I am trapped in.

He looks at me sharply. "You know me? I am not that famous."

I look at him helplessly. "The whole world knows you, General

Hannibal."

"Or will," I add feebly.

His gaze becomes even sharper, and I feel it cutting to my soul.

"General?" he asks. "You know much more or less than you say."

For a moment we stare at each other.

"I have given you shelter," he continues calmly. "I have offered you hospitality, and you have accepted it. While you are under my roof, I will do all in my power to keep you safe, for is that not the law of hospitality?"

I do not know what to say, and silence seems safer after the stupidity that escaped my mouth moments earlier.

"But," he adds, and now the sharpness in his eyes enters his voice, "If you prove to be a spy, you have violated those same rules of hospitality. I will throw you out of my home. Then I will kill you."

His last sentence is delivered flatly and without malice. He makes no dramatic gestures, like waving a dagger under my nose. But the simplicity just accentuates its implacable truth, like a law of nature, and I feel true fear. For how can I prove anything, if he chooses to distrust me?

I look at him with fresh eyes that now hold terror. For all that he has given me aid and shelter, and speaks as a civilized man: he is a warrior, born to a world of harsh violence; a man who will kill tens of thousands. What is one stranger's life worth to a man like this?

"I understand and accept, Hannibal son of Hamilcar. I swear I am no spy, and that I would never harm you, your city or your people."

We continue staring at each other, me trying to transmit sincerity, he trying to penetrate my secrets. Then I feel the tears pricking my eyes again, and with a mumbled apology I flee his presence.

Chapter 5: Hannibal

I watch her go.

Such a strange creature. Like a chimera, but a monster made not of mismatched animals but of equal parts beauty, mystery, impossible knowledge and equally impossible ignorance.

I warn myself to be careful, and think back on our interaction, searching for clues.

I had carried her back here, she never awakening from her faint. I had my slaves undress her and tend any wounds, then let her rest. I gave her a choice of clothes: hers or ours, knowing her choice would tell me something. She chose ours. So whatever the fineness of her raiment and its meaning to her, she does not feel compelled to wear it; nor does she despise our lesser offerings or wish to lord it over us. I had thought she would appear in her regalia. She proved me wrong, but I do not truly know what that means.

My slave told me she had woken and where she had gone, and I ordered her to bring the woman to me when she was ready.

Then she told me her name. Angela. The Greek word for Messenger or Herald, in its female form. In some religious texts, used to mean a messenger from the gods. Is that what she is? Not a goddess or priestess, but something in between, sent by the gods for their inscrutable purposes? But her manner is not right for the role: too much fear and too many tears. Could she be some lesser goddess, cast down from heaven by a more powerful deity and now living in fear, not understanding the mortal world and unable to return to the immortal? Again I chide myself for such thoughts: but I have no better theories.

A spy? I accused her of the same. But what kind of spy claims such ignorance in common matters yet reveals knowledge in deeper ones? What kind of spy, instead of flitting anonymously through the shadows, strides down the street in clothing fit for a queen? What kind of spy lacks knowledge of the language of the city she infiltrates, and speaks such execrable Greek as well?

Against all that is the simple fact that she not only knows my name but has successfully installed herself in my dwelling. Perhaps she is a more formidable adversary than appearances suggest, playing a game so subtle even I cannot see its bottom. For all her floundering, yet I feel danger in her, and hints of secret knowledge and power I cannot comprehend. What is she? Where is she from? Why is she unwilling or unable to answer?

Perhaps I should just kill her, for it would be easy enough to do. She is just a woman, unarmed and alone, with nobody to defend her life or her name. But something more than hospitality forbids me to think it. As much as I feel danger in her, I also feel promise and opportunity, though why is as obscure as the danger.

No, I will keep her here, play her friend, and see where she leads me. For now she is but a small yet mysterious piece in a complex game spanning nations, but whether she is a sacrificial pawn or the piece on which the game hinges is yet to be revealed. I shall set my slaves to watch her when I am not here, spies on a spy. Then I lean back, and sip my wine, and my thoughts turn to other matters.

CHAPTER 6: CARTHAGE

I have been here a month now. For a while, each time I opened my eyes in the morning I hoped they would open upon my previous life. I have given up that hope now. This is my life.

For the first time since my first morning, I put on my purple dress and its accompaniments, for today I am ready to ask my host for my second favor.

The first I asked for was on my second day, and I was dressed in the plain clothes of the household. It was a risky thing to ask for if Hannibal thought me a spy: but I needed it, and if he truly thought me a spy then nothing would save me.

I asked him for lessons: in contemporary Greek, Latin and his own language, the tongue of the Canaani. I knew Greek already, though I could tell from the puzzled and sometimes amused looks I received, and how his own accent appeared to my ears, that my accent was terrible and my knowledge incomplete. I was familiar with Latin too, but who in my modern age knew how it was properly spoken? The Roman Catholic church used to give their masses in Latin, quaintly imagining that worship in an unknown language was superior to one the congregation understood, but I was never Catholic. In any case I doubted my knowledge had suffered by being deprived of such an experience, as even the Church of Rome made up whatever pronunciation pleased them. As for Phoenician or Canaanite or whatever it was called, I had barely any knowledge at all.

Do you think three languages was ambitious? Merely staying alive was ambitious. Being able to speak was essential, and my choices were obvious. The language of my host and his people, so I could communicate with the inhabitants of this city, especially if I had to flee Hannibal; Greek, as the one I was most familiar with and therefore could hope to gain fluency in quickly, and spoken by many; Latin, as the language of Hannibal's, and perhaps therefore my, greatest enemy.

When I presented my request to Hannibal, for long moments he graced me with his chess-master stare. Then he said, "Tutors can be found. But how will you pay? You have no coin."

Thus was any doubt I may have had, as to whether my clothes and possibly my person had been searched while unconscious, dispelled.

"I have jewelry. Surely," I added, with more confidence in my voice than in my heart, "enough for the purpose."

Some further moves in the chess game flickered behind his eyes. "That will not be necessary. Your word will be sufficient surety. You may keep your gold and jewels until I call upon them. If you prove valuable enough to me, perhaps I will not need to."

I gave him my word, and applied myself with vigor to my studies as if my life depended on it. But in the back of my mind, his cryptic words about my value fermented with my own.

And so today I am ready. My skills of course are not even close to perfect, but they are greatly improved.

As I come up to my host he looks at me with surprise, but says nothing. I suppose any question is too obvious. But if he will not ask, I will let him wait. I sit, reach for an olive and chew it reflectively, glancing at him as if there is nothing strange about my presence or attire. Then before any impatience can manifest, I speak.

"My lord Hannibal," I begin. "You have had me hidden away here. I wish you to acknowledge my existence, and take me out to visit your city. Show me its grandeur, at your side."

"Dressed like that?"

"Dressed like this. Dressed as who I am."

"But who are you? Even I do not know that. For all I know, you could have fallen from the sky. Dressed plainly, you could pass as a servant, if anyone even noticed you. Dressed like that, no man would fail to notice. How would I explain your presence?"

"I believe you have spent much time in Spain, my lord, before your return here," I reply, eliciting an expression of surprise from him. "You could say I am a Spanish princess. That would explain both my wealth and my accent."

He studies me some more. "That could work, provided we encounter no men from Spain. Though if we do, they could be deflected. But why should I do this for you?"

"It is not only for me, Lord Hannibal. I believe it would benefit you too. It implies you have alliance with a powerful lord across the sea. Escort me around the city, pointing to its wonders; dressed like this, men would wonder. And the less you explain, the greater will be the mystery."

Hannibal smiles, one of the rare occasions when his smile directed at me contains warmth. "Perhaps I should fear a mind so subtle," he replies, and I am glad that his smile warms the words. "I agree to your request."

And so I am escorted out into the streets of Carthage by Hannibal. Despite my circumstances, the very thought thrills me to my bones. Here I am, a woman born in the late twentieth century, seeing the great Carthage on the arm of Hannibal himself! For once, it feels like a dream rather than a nightmare.

The city is not as grand as Rome must be, though it has regained at least some of the glory lost in its defeat a generation ago. Hannibal shows me the harbor, the great walls, the temples and more. If he still fears I am a spy, perhaps he knows I could have seen these things anyway; or perhaps, I feel with a new shiver of fear, he knows I will be unable to tell of them.

I know that Hannibal finds me intriguing; I do not know whether he likes me. I suspect it does not matter if he does. Hannibal is a great man, and great men are rarely kind men, usually not even nice men. If he decides I am a danger to his people or his ambitions, he will not hesitate to kill me. I cannot flee from him, for that would be a surer and possibly more unpleasant death. All I can do is try to earn his trust and hope he sees value in keeping me alive.

There are many temples, to many gods; these people seem to collect gods from other cultures to add to their own. As we walk down a street I am startled to see a familiar image on a wall: the image of a lamp with seven arms curving upwards. It looks like a menorah, the lamp that has great meaning to the Jews, and the Jewish link is strengthened by characters beneath it that look reminiscent of Hebrew.

I stop in surprise, the intrusion of the familiar into the distant past making me momentarily uncertain where I am. Hannibal sees the direction of my gaze. "Ah. You know of the people of Judah? They are our cousins, another tribe from our ancestral homeland in Canaan. But they hold themselves aloof. They despise the old gods, cleaving only to El. But we are a free people. As long as they remain wise enough to keep their opinions private and not blaspheme our gods in public, they are free to worship as they please. If the gods are offended by it, I am sure the gods will have their vengeance without our help."

I don't recall anything about there being Jews in ancient Carthage, but, as Hannibal said, they are cousins to the Phoenicians, and with the poor records and coming ruin of the entire city, it isn't surprising that this small presence was lost to history. But his words chill me when I think of the coming fate of that people, from the Romans to the Nazis and innumerable persecutions in between. *The gods will have their vengeance*. Perhaps they did.

We move on, and we come upon the great temple of Baal-Hamon, lord of storms, god of weather and fertility, the chief god of Carthage. Nearby is the temple of his consort Tanit, goddess of the moon and of war, virgin mother goddess, symbol of fertility.

But if she is a symbol of motherhood and fertility, she also has a darker side. Hannibal points to where children are sacrificed to these terrible deities, like a tour guide explaining some spot of picturesque interest. He evinces no shame at this practice, but nor does he show enthusiasm; he merely remarks that children are sacrificed there when special favors are needed or granted from the gods: many already dead, but some still living. I hide my revulsion, fearing giving offense, knowing that nowhere in the ancient world is it safe to display a negative judgement of the gods and their inscrutable demands.

I ask to stand for a while, as I look out over the temple and city, and at the man who escorts me. If he suspects why I must stop, and why I shake, he says nothing. In so many ways these people seem civilized. I remember Ricky, extolling their virtues as the great empire of trade not conquest. Yet they burn their children for their gods. A tear escapes my eye, perhaps in sadness at the loss of a dream, perhaps for the children.

Then I think of all the other barbarities of the ancient world. I remember that child sacrifice was not unknown, neither in other tribes of Canaan, not even in Israel itself at times; nor elsewhere around the world. I think of the slaves, not only here but in Rome as well, indeed everywhere: the victims of war or raids, plucked from their homes and their lives, now the property of others. I think of the Roman games.

The casual brutality.

I wish I was not here.

But I know that I cannot truly judge these people, any of them. It is so easy, to stand on the pinnacle we have reached, and look down on the practices of our ancestors. Yet were we born here, would we have been any different?

"I think I have seen enough for one day," I whisper to Hannibal, suddenly too tired to continue. He nods, his thoughts hidden from me, and we leave this place. But as we walk, he releases one of his thoughts in answer to mine.

"We all die, Angela, and we all journey to the land of Mot. Perhaps a death for a purpose is a better death than that of so many who die to no purpose. Perhaps being taken to the bosom of the Mother is a blessing, however many tears we may shed for our loss."

I nod. But I do not think the image in my mind of burning children will ever leave me.

CHAPTER 7: HANNIBAL

It is time to go.

I have found many good men and in two days I will be taking them, my cargo and my ships home to Iberia.

I have not yet decided what to do with the woman, Angela. Angel or demon, innocent or spy? Her skill with languages is impressive, but with her fluent tongue has not come any fluent explanations. Still she claims not to know how she arrived here; still she says she does not know in what direction her home lies. When I ask her to describe it to me, she says she cannot. When I ask why she cannot, she tells me she will not lie to me, and if she told the truth I would believe her mad.

Whatever profit I gained from the mystery she raises in others' minds is a loss in my own.

But surely the first talent of a spy is lies.

I call her to me and tell her I am leaving the day after tomorrow. A flash of fear flickers in her eyes, possibly because she now knows the difference between 'I' and 'we'. I can see the thoughts behind those eyes; I only wish that were true of all the thoughts she hides from me. She is afraid that I will simply kill her, that I am unwilling to let an enigma like her live in such dangerous and treacherous times. She is afraid that I will simply go, leaving her alone in the city; perhaps she would survive, but more likely, having been abandoned by her protector, she would be taken by my enemies and enslaved, raped, tortured, killed, or all of those fates.

I see the fear begin its change to pleading, and I look away. It is not that I need to hide from her sight. It is that I cannot help her, and there is nothing to say.

"My lord," she says. There is pleading in her voice, yes. But there is also resolve; and a thread of reckless iron, as if she knows her life is in the balance and she dares risk all on a single throw. Pleading I can ignore, but courage deserves respect, and I turn to face her.

"Take me with you."

I am surprised, not by the request, but that her tone is not of a plea, but an offer. I simply look at her, waiting.

"Lord Hannibal, I swear I am not a spy. I swear I would never betray you, just as you would never betray your people. I cannot tell you where I am from. My vision is murky, but I know some of the past, and some of the future: not because I am a spy, but because of what I am. I know you have sworn an oath to never be a friend of Rome, as I now swear an oath that I will ever be your friend. I know you have been planning to fight Rome, to attack the Romans on their own soil. I know you would even cross the mountains with elephants to do it. I know you will win great victories."

She pauses, as if frightened to continue. I stare at her, daring her to continue despite her fear.

"I know that despite all that, you will lose. That Carthage itself will fall. I do not know that I can help you. But I know that without me, that is your fate, and the fate of your people."

She closes her eyes, as if expecting me to end her life here and now. I am sorely tempted to oblige her. How does she know so much, if she is not a spy? How could I risk letting her live?

But the weapons of a spy are stealth, a dagger in the night, poison; perhaps seduction. In all the time she has been with me, she has attempted none of them, nor been free to practice them on others. Her fate hangs in the balance; but perhaps so does mine.

A messenger of the gods? I wonder again. But is the trap to believe her? Or to spurn her? Gods or men, spy or savior, how can I see to the bottom of such roiling depths as these?

My decision rests on a knife edge. Still she sits, her eyes closed waiting for the blow; a lone tear escaping from them as proof that, amidst all else she is or may be, she is still a woman, lost and alone. To kill her is the obvious choice, but it is not my way to take the obvious choices. She has risked all on this gambit. And that is my way too: to dare, to throw my challenge to the gods themselves; and in daring, to win.

"I have one condition."

Her eyes fly open. "Name it."

She is still a woman, lost and alone.

"You may come with me... as my wife."

"What? What...?"

She stares at me helplessly, perhaps wondering if I jest. Finally she whispers, "Why?"

"Do you not think a man could desire you?"

"But... yes... no... I mean, you have never shown any... I mean, you are a man, but... I..."

I am amused. She has not been this incoherent since her appalling Greek the first time she opened her mouth in my city.

"Do not worry, if you fear a man's desire. Though I warn you that if you do, as my wife you will have to bear it. But I have two reasons besides. The first is practical: it gives me a good reason to take you with me, one nobody would question."

"And... and the second?"

"If the gods wish to play with me and send me their angel or a goddess herself, then I shall grasp their dare with both hands and leap it, like a Cretan over a bull! If the gods wish to test Hannibal son of Hamilcar the Lightning, then I shall not run and I shall not quail, but shall double the stakes and throw their game in their face!"

~~~

I lie on my bed, staring into the night. I still cannot believe my fate.

I chose a Spanish princess as my cover story not only because it explained my exotic nature, but because I knew Hannibal had married one. The implication that has now rocked me to my core never occurred to me. Little is recorded in history about Hannibal's wife. I had hoped for no more than camouflage: that any tales that might spread of my time here with Hannibal would simply be confused with tales of his later wife: my intrusion into the past safely buried, the timeline of history left unblemished.

It also didn't occur to me because history reports his wife's name was Imilce, albeit not from a notably dependable source. Then I think of my own name, Angela Milton, A. Milton, and think how often in history words and names are corrupted from their actual form to a more familiar one. I wonder if the source was more reliable than we imagined, and I am indeed her. Whether perhaps she was always me.

How can we know when we are dreaming? When we are awake it

is easy enough to tell and we can smile at the folly of our dreams. But it is a different matter when we are still inside them. Maybe I should have spent more time in philosophy classes, though from what experience I do have it would not have helped me. It is a rare philosopher who admits they know anything or can help you know anything. Their only absolute is when your assignment is late. Or if it comes to a question of their salary, upon which emergency they acquire a more laser-like identification of reality than they grant to the Earth on which they walk. If I could have invoked one of them to stand before me, what would he have said? Probably that you cannot invoke a philosopher out of thin air like that, and his very existence in front of me proves he does not in fact exist.

I smile at the thought that imaginary philosophers are starting to make more sense than actual ones. But this does not help me know whether I am dreaming, for no philosopher actually appears to scold me. No philosopher appears to give me the touchstone to decide between dream and reality, whichever state I am in. No philosopher appears to tell me how I can become Hannibal's wife in my own distant past, or even whether such an absurdity coming to pass is itself the proof I seek.

It is all too much for my mind to understand or accept, and it escapes into the peace of sleep. Or perhaps it merely exchanges one dream for another.

CHAPTER 8: THE CROSSING

I stand on the stern of the ship, looking back at Carthage as we sail away. I am wearing my purple. I see many people watching us go; feel many wondering eyes upon me.

I laugh at their stares. Even more, I laugh at the thought of Hannibal's proposal. Truly, I had simply hoped that any word of my presence in Carthage at Hannibal's side would, in the misty wash of rumor and history, merge with the vague tales of his marriage to a Spanish princess. I do not know if any of this real, but I feel that my best hope of staying alive is to change recorded history as little as possible. Like one of those moths that look like the bark of the trees they rest on, invisibility is the key to life. I never dreamed that my camouflage would become my reality.

I have an idea that sends me a surge of reckless amusement. I do not know why I do it, only that it feels right. No, that is not true. Whatever mystique has grown about me, I wish it to grow more. And so I face the city and raise my arms above my head like a goddess bringing down a blessing upon Carthage. I stand that way until the city is just a smudge in the distance.

I wonder who was watching and what they made of the sight. Perhaps word of it will one day reach Rome itself. It is a small gesture, but sometimes the accumulation of such small gestures can tip the balance and move the world.

Still I wonder whether it was wisdom or folly that made me do it.

~~~

The Phoenicians were mighty mariners, born to sail the open sea. It does not take long for me to discover I am a pretender to the title. As the ship rolls on the waves, I begin to feel the stirrings of seasickness.

As Hannibal's betrothed, I have a private area drawn aside for me, and I decide my reputation is best served by mysteriously withdrawing to it in order to mysteriously commune with the gods for a while. I feel my imagined mystique might be tarnished by the sight of me leaning over the side feeding the fishes with my breakfast.

Fortunately, after a while my stomach begins to settle, and I think I can move about without risking an embarrassing incident. I have just sat up when I hear a commotion outside. I hurry to the deck and see men shouting and pointing. I gather that there has been an accident. In the confusion of shouting it is not clear to me exactly what happened, but a man has fallen overboard, hitting his head somewhere in the process, and has been lost to the sea. The waves that had been disturbing my stomach are still rather rough and foaming, and it is hard to see where the man might be, assuming he is not already taken by its depths. But then someone cries out and points. He is found! But he is now some distance from the ship and not moving. Two of the men jump into the water and strike out to try to rescue him.

They are fine swimmers, as one might hope for a seafaring people, but I fear their breast-stroke style will prove too slow. Almost without thinking, I cast off my outer gown and leap into the water. I am a strong swimmer, using the overarm stroke honed by centuries of competition, and I quickly overtake the others; and I am lucky, for I manage to reach the man before he slips permanently into the deep. As it is, he begins to sink before I can get him and I must dive beneath the water to retrieve his body. He is unconscious and I drag him back, now swimming side stroke, my other hand cupping his chin to keep his head above the water. By the time I reach the two sailors I am tiring, and they help us all back to the ship and safety.

The men of the ship stare at me as we climb on board, though whether in surprise at what I did or in shock at my near nakedness I do not know. I am too exhausted to care. But when they lay the victim on deck and examine him, one looks my way with sadness in his eyes. "A valiant effort, my lady. But it is too late: there is no longer breath in him."

"No!" I cry. I will not accept this, and kneel by his side, doing what I can to clear his throat and pump the water from his lungs. I feel his wrist, but there is no pulse. Automatically, I begin standard resuscitation techniques. Alternately I breathe into his mouth and pump his chest with my hands. I begin to feel the man was right and I am too late; but before the despair of failure makes me stop he coughs, more water spews from his mouth, and his eyes flicker open.

I stagger to my feet, worn from my efforts, and command, "Dry him, wrap him in warm clothes, and give him some hot broth! And keep him warm!"

The men say nothing, staring at me with eyes even wider than when I climbed back on board: but they obey. Drained, I sit weakly on a barrel, barely noticing when one of the men gently drapes my robe over my shoulders. I see that Hannibal is watching me; for once I seem to have startled even him. Slowly he walks toward me; then he reaches out his hand, takes mine, and draws me to my feet. Then he leads me away, turns me to face him, and again stares into my face.

"What manner of woman are you?" he asks hoarsely. "That you can swim like a fish and breathe life back into the dead?"

I shake my head. "He was not dead. Not yet. Else even I could not have brought him back."

He just gapes at me, for once lost for words; for once even the chess master behind his eyes silenced by a move too unexpected to understand.

~~~

For the rest of the crossing the men of the ship avoid me, avoid my eyes when I pass. It is as if they fear that if I can give life with a breath and a touch, perhaps I can take it as easily with a glance. They treat me with respect; not like the respect they have for Hannibal, which is the respect of men for a leader who has proven himself, but with the respect they would show a dangerous power, one neither to be understood nor hindered. Even Hannibal is not immune, his usually polite reserve shaded with something akin to wonder.

There is one exception: the man I saved, whose name I learn is Barekbaal. When he recovered he sought me out and prostrated himself before me. "My lady," he said, "I have heard what you did. You returned my life to me after it had fled my body. Thus I give the rest of that life to you. If you will accept me I shall defend you to the death, and serve you for all the days you have given me. If you reject me, throw me back into the waves' embrace."

And so I acquire a servant, a bodyguard, perhaps even a friend beneath the awe. Hannibal does not forbid it, telling Barekbaal that he will serve Hannibal as well by my side as elsewhere; cryptically telling me, "It is good that you are watched." I do not know whether he wants me watched over or simply watched, and he does not enlighten me.

Our destination is a new town with the imaginative name of 'New Town' (it sounds more exotic in Phoenician), on the coast of Spain, or Iberia as it is known in this time. 'New Town' is not only unimaginative but confusing, as it is named after Carthage, which itself simply means 'New Town'. In my own mind I insist on calling it New Carthage so I know which city I'm thinking about, knowing that will become its name in due course. Indeed the city will still exist in my own time, its name morphed into Cartagena, and after all those millennia it will remain an important port.

This morning we at last sail into New Carthage. I have lived in fear of my life for so long; now with the warm Mediterranean sun shining, and a cool wind from the sea blowing my hair, at last I feel hope.

CHAPTER 9: THE BRIDE

We have been in New Carthage for two weeks now.

Our, or should I say Hannibal's, arrival was greeted with much cheer. My appearance at his side was greeted with much amazement; when they learned I was to be his bride, there was much celebration.

There were days of greeting old friends and feasting. Here in Spain we did not claim that I was a Spanish princess, but that is what our sailors believed and we happily allowed the rumors to flourish. There were many guesses as to which city was my home and which king my father; we did not answer them. There was whispered speculation as to why my kingly father or his family had made no appearance yet, despite our approaching wedding. Perhaps my family had been wiped out in one of the various wars; perhaps Hannibal himself had slain my family but been smitten by my exotic beauty and spared my life; or no, he had slain those who had murdered my family and saved me. Or perhaps my father was an enemy king, and Hannibal had stolen me away in a daring night time raid.

It was all very romantic, if total twaddle.

If anybody tried to speak to me in a Spanish dialect, I merely smiled and answered in Phoenician that I was Hannibal's now and I intended to speak his language.

The story of Barekbaal's return to life also spread through the city, and so rumors that I was some High Priestess lending the aid of the gods to Hannibal fought with the rumors that I was a rescued Princess.

"I told you I could be useful to you," I said to Hannibal once. His only reply was a smile.

So now my wedding day has come. I was not nervous until today, not about the wedding. It was too unreal; too outside the bounds of possibility to do more than glide off the surface of my mind whenever I thought about it. If I was nervous, it was about the possibility that I would in fact never live to see my wedding night; farther from home and friends than can be imagined, at the mercy of a warrior who had little cause to trust me.

But no poison slipped between my lips and no knife slipped between my ribs, and here I am.

I have not been staying with Hannibal. Though that is what I did in Carthage, now I am to be his bride we have been living apart, guards outside and loyal Barekbaal inside as my protectors, and with a bevy of servants as my chaperones. But today I am to leave here and be taken to Hannibal's house, there to begin my new life.

I will not wear my purple today. Today I become Hannibal's, and so for now I put aside my old life. I am dressed in a white gown, beautifully decorated with gold and pearls; a band of deep purple around the hem and arms. Servants have spent a long time on my person, and my skin glows, and my hair shines as it cascades down my body in gold-adorned waves. Garlands of scented flowers hang over my shoulders.

Even I think I am beautiful today.

Hannibal is even more beautiful. He is dressed like a king, from the braided sandals on his feet past the silk sash around his waist to the gold crown on his head. I find it amusing that this hard man renowned through the centuries as a warrior is wearing clothes scented like a perfume shop, but I keep my mirth to myself.

My faithful Barekbaal looks on. I do not have to worry about jealousy. Even if he dared be jealous of Hannibal, he shows no sign of thinking of me as a sexual being. To him I am a force of nature, beyond considerations of the flesh; to be adored, but not coveted; with whom unwanted attentions would and should be met with deadly wrath.

There is celebration and drinking and merriment and vows, as we are joined together as husband and wife. I do not remember much of the time. I remember only that I lived it, and I will never see its like again.

I have not had sex since my night with Ricky, though I don't know whether that means my abstinence should be measured in months or millennia. So as the moment that defines the first night of any married couple's life approaches, I can feel the anticipation in my bones and my more personal parts, but it is anticipation leavened with fear. The last time I had sex I was hurled out of my own time: what will happen tonight? Might I snap back to my own age, to awaken where I started and be left forever wondering whether this was all a dream? Or worse, what if I am cursed to jump back through the millennia, until I die alone in some Stone Age swamp?

Finally I am led to Hannibal's bedchamber. This is one place Barekbaal will not follow.

I look at him in awe at what I am about to do; the truth that I am about to lie with the great Hannibal finally and inescapably real. He looks back at me, for once his eyes saying the same as mine; for the second time in our life the chessboard of stratagems swept away and forgotten. Perhaps he wonders whether I am a god, and our union will consume him until nothing is left but ash. But he can no more stop it than I can. We move together, and suddenly I am wrapped in his arms, his mouth upon mine.

I am so used to his cool calculations and words of calm death that to feel him give way to passion, to raw desire for me as a woman, shocks me. But give way it does, and I feel my clothes stripped from my body, our rich gowns discarded like so many rags, his hard body pressing against my soft flesh. And then I am on the bed, and there is a man above me, and I feel the driving of his passion, and the driving goes on and on until I know nothing but the driving, until the waves of pleasure make me cry out in joy or pain, and we lie together, gasping and complete.

And as I hold him and he holds me, our sweat mingling, I know that we are become one. And so I drift off to sleep, with the one thought in my mind: I am still here.

~~~

I wake the next morning.

I am still here.

Perhaps I should be disappointed. But I deserve my honeymoon, surely. I look at Hannibal sleeping beside me and savor the word in my mind: *husband*. It feels so strange, to be a wife. Yet oddly, so right, even though I am a woman so far out of her time.

Then he wakes, and smiles at me, for once his smile one of simple happiness and acceptance. We have great things to do, this man and I.

No doubt he has many important tasks awaiting his attention even now.

But he too feels that we have reached some sought for oasis, are living in a bubble of time, for this moment free from the concerns of the world and of history and of destiny.

I reach out for him, and we do it again.

And I am still here.

Chapter 10: Hasdrubal

It is a sunny day in New Town as I walk the walls of the city. The city I founded. I still feel a surge of pride when I stand on the walls and survey its buildings and streets. It is a fine port, and perhaps one day it will rival even Carthage in glory.

I lean on a rampart as I look out over the city and think about its future. I have worked hard to extend our people's influence in the north. And we are growing. When my wife's father, the great Hamilcar, came to Iberia, Carthage's power had sunk so low that he had to cross at the narrow straits to the west, so reduced were the number of ships available to him. In the seven years since Hamilcar's untimely death in war and my appointment in his place, I have built New Town and extended our influence more by peace than by war: by treaty rather than conquest. Thus we distinguish ourselves from the Romans, who seek only to rule and take tribute from their conquests, to fatten themselves at the world's expense.

Even with the Romans I have made peace. They are Romans, and the peace cannot last: but I have my own plans for them. They will find that although we Canaani prefer trade and the peace it thrives upon, we are not afraid of war when it is necessary.

This leads my thoughts to Hannibal, Hamilcar's eldest son, my brother. He was but a lad, not even twenty years old, when his father died: too young to inherit his father's command. That is why it is mine, not his. I am glad he has made it safely back from Carthage. He has his father's look about him, that one, nor am I the first or only one to make note of it. And more: I see the genius of the gods in him, a talent for strategy and war that has few equals. What is it that is written in the books of wisdom of our brothers, the people of Judah? There is a time for peace, and a time for war? Perhaps when the time of peace is over and the time of war is upon us, it is Hannibal not I who will finish the great task begun by his father and built up by me.

I wonder about his bride, the mysterious Angela. Hannibal and I are best friends, but either he hides the truth about her from me or he does not know it himself. Some call her a witch: but they do so quietly, when they think none can hear. But most think her a messenger from the gods, a sign of the gods' favor upon our people. And it seems to be so. For what witch saves a man's life, unbidden; and what witch, having done so, would not extract some terrible price from her victim? Yet Barekbaal loves her, seeming neither bewitched nor resentful. Those who whisper that Angela is a witch are in more danger from him than from her.

Part of me fears for Hannibal and that his alliance with this woman, let alone one so intimate, might lead to his destruction, like a man attempting to harness the power of a gorgon. But the greater part of me knows that Hannibal is a force equal to any the gods may throw at him, and that whatever she or the gods themselves might seek to gain by their union, if any man could turn it to his advantage it is Hannibal.

But these are matters for the future, and I descend to the streets and the present. As we walk through the town, a man in rough and dusty clothes stumbles into my path. I stop, and cry out, "Stranger, what ails you?"

He turns to me and replies, "What ails me? What ails me is that my master Tago is dead!"

And with that he whips out a dagger, and before I can react, thrusts it into my belly.

I fall back, staring at him in shock. My men grab him, but he does not struggle. Instead he laughs, as if none can now touch him. "Join him now, oh great Hasdrubal!" he sneers. "You who are so mighty, who think you can slay any you please, learn that you are as mortal!"

I cannot speak. I can feel my life ebbing, can see my world darkening at its edges. I look into the eyes of my enemy, eyes filled with equal parts hate and triumph, and wonder about this man Tago for whom I die. He died in war, did he not? As did the great Hamilcar, the father of my wife who is about to be my widow. Is that not the choice we men make? To fight, risking all to gain all, rather than accept the peace of obscurity or surrender? Did not this Tago make the same choice, no doubt killing many others before his own time claimed him? So where is the justice this man seeks?

I feel the ashes of defeat in my mouth, to die in such a way, not in the heat of war but in the streets of my own city: my great task yet unfinished. I can only hope that I have done enough, and that others can finish what I have begun.

I hope Hannibal is ready.

I hope.

I die.

Chapter 11: Hannibal

D isaster!
        Word came this morning. There was a commotion at the door, and I leapt up to deal with it.

When my father Hamilcar died in battle, my brother in law Hasdrubal, more than a score years older than I, took command in Iberia. After my return and my marriage, he sent me out of New Town to an important but smaller garrison farther along the coast, where I was tasked with improving the fortifications and recruiting and training more soldiers. So there I went with my new wife and made my home, expecting to be away for some time.

Now Hasdrubal is dead, slain by an assassin!

When I hear the news, I rush back to my wife.

"My brother, fair Hasdrubal, is slain," I inform her. "Murdered by a slave avenging his master! I must return to New Town. Today."

She sits up in bed, her face ashen. "Then I shall go with you."

She is a strange one, my new wife Angela, her manner hard to understand. Occasionally I think she must have been the High Priestess of some cult, for she is unafraid of men and speaks her mind without fear. Yet it is not as if she is used to command: her manner is not that of one practiced at giving orders, simply one used to speaking her mind among equals and expecting to be heard.

I am taken aback by her immediate assumption that attending to such a matter as this is something on which she should accompany me. But as I have said, she is a strange one, and her powers as mysterious as her true origins.

As we travel, I tell her about Hasdrubal. Hasdrubal the Fair they call him, and he was fair in more than appearance. He was a true son of Carthage: it is he who founded New Town, and since he took over from my father he has expanded and solidified Carthage's power and wealth in Iberia. And while unafraid of battle his chief weapon was diplomacy with the natives; he even made treaty with the Romans, knowing we were not ready for conflict with such a power. Who can imagine what he might have accomplished had he lived? Truly it is a great tragedy that he is gone, and all for the misguided loyalty of a slave, who will soon enough meet his own more fitting end.

Even her manner of listening to my tale is strange. She listens with intense interest, yet it is as if some of what I say is already known to her, other parts are unknown, and yet others surprise her as if they are particularly unexpected: even though I expect her to know none of the history of my family in Iberia, and there is nothing especially unusual about the things which surprise her.

When we arrive in New Town, I tell her to remain where she can see and hear but not be seen.

"Why?" she asks. As I said, she is strange, questioning even me. But I am not angry. Her sibylline power is why I want her near; why I married her. Priestess or god or something even stranger, I am now linked to that power, and its flames have not consumed me yet.

"There are many rumors about you, Angela. But while we encourage them, you must not be seen to control me, for that would lead to far more dangerous whisperings. So for this, stay in the background. Hasdrubal is dead; what I do about it must be seen to be mine."

She nods. Again that strange mixture: she is neither headstrong and defiant nor meekly obedient: but having asked for my reasons and heard them, simply accepts them.

And so she stays behind in her plain travelling clothes, while I climb to where I can address the army, still in shock and angry mourning over Hasdrubal.

"Hasdrubal, the mighty, the fair, the glorious, is no more!" I cry to them. "But what he has done will live on for the rest of time! Here we stand in the city he founded; here we mourn his death; but from here we shall build on his legacy, and spread the power and glory of Carthage throughout the world!"

A great shout comes from the crowd.

"Hasdrubal! Hasdrubal!" they cry in tribute.

"But to achieve his legacy we must move on!" I cry in reply. "We need to choose a leader to replace him and continue the work so cruelly cut off! So consider among yourselves, put forward the names of those you think worthy, and together we will decide!"

"There is no need!" shouts a lone voice from the edges of the crowd. Then one, then many, then all begin to shout my name: "Hannibal! Hannibal! Hannibal!"

It is a heady moment, to stand above a crowd of men and warriors, all crying your name in affirmation.

And so out of this tragedy I achieve my ambition and become leader of the army in Iberia. It is not the way I would have chosen to achieve it. But when the gods decide to grant our wishes they have no concern with the price we might be willing to pay for it, and impose whatever price that amuses them: and we can only hope it is not too cruel. This price is high indeed, but to refuse the gift would only anger the gods, for no gain and more pain, while the price remained forever paid.

Of course I am not the king of my own city but a citizen of Carthage. My appointment cannot come from acclamation alone, not even the acclamation of an army: the Great Ones of Carthage must approve it. But given my heritage, the distance and the support of the soldiers, I do not expect any difficulty, not even amidst the often muddy ambitions and loyalties that swirl in any government.

~~~

When the confirmation arrives from Carthage I show it to Angela. "When we met, you mistakenly called me 'General'," I say with a smile. "At the time I did not know whether you were a spy, mistaken, a flatterer or a prophet. Whatever you are, now it is true."

She smiles back but does not answer.

I still do not know.

CHAPTER 12: ANGELA

My husband Hannibal has been busy.

Those words, 'my husband Hannibal', still send a shiver down my spine, at once such a normal description of my life and a thing so astounding I can only stare at the concept without understanding or judgement. I might be looking at him as we share a meal. Or hearing his voice as we discuss the minutiae of running a household, as husbands and wives have done for millennia and perhaps always will. Or looking at him dreamily after he has shared my bed. Then those words will come to me, and I will roll them around in my mind; and all else will vanish in their quotidian enormity.

Yet even now after more than a year here, I cannot allow myself to believe my new life is real. I still cling to the hope that if I refuse to acknowledge it, one morning I will awake to my original life; I still hold the fear that if I once believe it, I will be lost down this rabbit hole forever. So I have maintained a kind of cynical pragmatism about it all. I will eat my breakfast, jump out of the way of ox carts, and otherwise act as I would as if the world around me were real: but the reality itself, that I will scorn.

If I am going to eat imaginary food and enjoy imaginary sex, I am also going to do the other things my nature demands as I live my imaginary life. And I am a historian who finds herself on an unexpected field trip, even if it might be only in my mind. Strangely for a people who had such an influence on history, relatively little is known about the Phoenicians and their culture. There is the occasional monument carved in stone, and more or less reliable reports about them from other cultures, often their enemies. But of their daily lives and their culture in their own words, there is more ignorance and speculation than knowledge. It is an ironic fate for the culture who spread their alphabet around the Mediterranean, thus becoming an ancestor of most alphabets from ancient times to the modern day, to leave so few of their own written records in their wake.

The main reason for this dearth of information is that while they wrote a lot, they wrote it on papyrus. In fact their oldest city, believed by many to be the oldest inhabited city in the world, was named Byblos after its trade in papyrus from Egypt. Papyrus has its virtues, but being archival quality isn't one of them. This famous precursor of paper was invented by the Egyptians, who made it from the pith of Nile reeds thinly cut into strips, laid down in parallel and held together by pressing them onto other strips placed at right angles. Papyrus is one of those inventions that transformed the world. But as you can probably imagine, such a material is fragile, and in humid environments, like the places frequented by the Phoenicians, it rapidly decays. So papyrus records buried in some arid desert or dry cave might last centuries or millennia and give archaeologists things to argue about for similar lengths of time, but mere tantalizing fragments remain from the Phoenicians.

I must remain true to myself even, or perhaps especially, in a fantasy world, lest I lose myself entirely. So given an opportunity like this I must grasp it: I will observe the world of the Phoenicians and record the facts about their civilization. One day, when the time and place is right, I will seal my work as best I can and store it in a dry place that should survive the ravages of time. And hope that one day some archaeologist will stumble upon my treasure. I might have gotten away with papyrus if I had stored it carefully, but there is a better option. Parchment, made from the stretched and dried skin of young animals, is much more robust. It is also easier to write upon, being large smooth sheets rather than joined strips. So it is parchment that my heart sets itself upon.

Did I say that Hannibal has been busy? His policy is simple and logical. He knows Rome is his greatest threat, and that to resist Rome his people need a strong foundation. So he has embarked on completing the absorption of Spain into the Carthaginian empire. I do not accompany him on his military adventures. I am a woman of the twenty first century, and the violence of this one appalls me. Do not misunderstand. The people of a later age should not judge those of an earlier one by their own standards, unless they have enough arrogance to presume they would have acted any differently. I understand why Hannibal does what he does; I even agree that it is needed. While conquest is not really the Phoenician way, when faced with an enemy like Rome it is necessary. And it is not as if those he conquers treat their own neighbors or even their own people any better. I am not so foolish as to imagine that this era suffers the conquest of the peaceful by the violent: rather it is the defeat of the violent by the more effectively violent. I can only hope—indeed, I truly believe—that the end result will be more peace and prosperity, not less.

But still I cannot yet watch these events with equanimity. I see Hannibal, indeed the Phoenicians as a people, as civilized and good. My heart cannot watch them slaughter others, no matter how my head thinks it is beyond my power or my right to stop it. In my heart I fear, or perhaps know, that one day I will have to join Hannibal in his wars. That day is not yet.

So I let him go to fight his wars, and I support him as a wife is expected to, and hope that I am better than all those others who throughout history have kept silent, closing their eyes and refusing to speak for the dispossessed and the dead.

Do you think that these are strange thoughts for a historian? Maybe you are right. But there is more to history than wars and the rise and fall of cities. They are important, yes. Hannibal has taken cities and brought much booty to Carthage, honing and displaying his battlefield prowess. But my world already knows these things, and I do not think it will gain much by learning more literally gory details about Hannibal's campaigns in Spain. My goal is not to paint in details of the known but to shine a light on the forgotten.

The morning after Hannibal's latest return home, I approach him.

"Husband," I say to him, "Could you get me some scrolls of parchment to write on?"

At least he no longer looks at me with those chess master eyes when I make requests like this. The chess master must have long decided that my moves are never going to make much sense, so he might as well just lean back and watch my antics with detached bemusement until a clearer pattern emerges from the chaos.

"Why can't you use papyrus like everyone else? It's a lot cheaper. For that matter, what do you have to write so much about anyway?"

"Parchment is a lot more durable than papyrus."

"So what do you have to write that has to be so durable?"

"The story of your people, so that the men of the future will know your full glory. Your beliefs, your daily lives, your philosophy and knowledge."

The chess master suddenly discovers an interest in our conversation. "That implies you expect all that will be lost. Now why do you think that?"

"Because you all write everything on papyrus!"

He sends me a dire look. I doubt he has forgotten what I said about the demise of Carthage early on, and I can see him putting that with what I have just said. Then the glint in his eyes changes to one of amusement and he gives a short laugh. "If I demand you tell me exactly what you're talking about, I'm not going to get a straight answer, am I?"

I grace him with a look I hope is both haughty and mysterious, and say nothing.

"That's what I thought." He sighs. "But it isn't worth fighting over. I will get you your parchment."

And so my great project begins.

I will write in Greek, knowing the language will be known to my hypothetical discoverers. I will write about their customs, their religion, their politics, their philosophy, their virtues and vices. I find the prospect so exciting that it thrills me despite my skepticism of whether I am writing anything at all outside the vaults of my own mind.

~~~

This morning I am recording my thoughts and cheerfully thinking about the service I am performing for historians when I pause. I realize I am an idiot. If all this is a fever dream then I am writing for nobody. If against all probability and sanity this is real, then how am I here to see it and record it? Talk about the specialist's tunnel vision! Recording the titbits of a dead civilization for unborn historians and coffee table books, while forgetting the little matter of being blasted more than two millennia back in time, and what that could mean for science.

So I must record that too. But I do not wish to be thought mad or dangerous if someone here happens to read my work; nor do I wish my work to be lumped with myths and legends upon its discovery, relegating me from time traveler to primitive novelist. The solution is obvious: I will write those parts in English. Now *that* would shock my future discoverers, especially when their carbon dating proves I wrote it centuries before Christ!

But what if English never exists in the new timeline? I cannot believe I am really here, and even if I am I don't know whether my presence will change recorded history in any way. Yet if I am going to all this trouble, I might as well account for the possibilities. So what if my actions here do change history, and in such a way that the English language is different, or perhaps never even arises? I remember the impossibility of deciphering hieroglyphics until the Rosetta Stone was discovered, with its duplicated texts in languages known and unknown. Imagine the irony of recording this staggering scientific discovery (accidental as it is), only to have my archive become unintelligible gibberish because the discovery is even greater than I thought possible: to not merely travel in time, but to change it!

So I shall include my own Rosetta Stone.

I read back over my scroll. Yes, there should be enough variety in this long section for the cryptologists of the future. So I take my pen and draw a distinctive frame around the passage. Now I translate it into English. It takes a while but I am happy with the result, and I draw the same frame around the English version.

If that isn't a big enough clue for my future colleagues, then I despair for their intelligence.

I will keep my two tales separate. So I put aside my current scroll for continuing my history later and begin a new one, with a shorter key as some insurance against separation or loss of the other. And thus I begin my tale of the woman who travelled through time, the history of the world as I knew it in my own era, the reality of the world I found myself in: and perhaps, the beginning of the history of the world as it will now become.

CHAPTER 13: ANGELA

Hannibal's elephants are a sight to amaze.

They are funny elephants, smaller than I imagined. When I think of elephants from Africa, I think of the giants of the elephant world. But apparently those ones have tempers to match their size and are not easily subjugated to man. These are a smaller species from North Africa, more tractable. They are even a bit smaller than Indian elephants. If you wonder how I know so much about elephants, it is simply because there appear to be a couple of the Indian versions, brought from the Middle East, here among their company for comparison. But 'small' is relative when it comes to elephants, and I would not like to be a Roman legionary facing this army of tusked behemoths. Hannibal himself is quite a magnificent sight perched on top of one of the larger beasts. I am sure it impresses his allies as much as it will terrorize his foes.

But the sight makes me uneasy, for I know the end of that road.

Hannibal's predecessor, Hasdrubal known as the Fair, had not only embarked on a campaign to bring Iberia under Carthaginian sway but had signed a peace treaty with Rome. Carthage would stay south of the great Spanish river Ebro and Rome would stay north. Rome honored this bargain—in a fashion more suited to a nation of lawyers than warriors. They did not cross the Ebro, but made the city of Saguntum, well south of the river, their protectorate, allegedly because they were asked to by its inhabitants.

I was tempted to counsel Hannibal to let it be, but I knew he would not listen in the face of such provocation. He duly laid siege to the city, and it duly fell to his armies.

In the usual hypocritical irony of diplomacy and wars, the Roman Senate complained that the taking of 'their' city was a violation of the treaty, though of course Hannibal regarded them making it a Roman protectorate in the first place as the violation. The Romans took their complaint to Carthage, but Carthage would not be baited into either declaring war or choosing a peace with undoubted undesirable consequences. They said Rome could decide. The Romans, presumably to nobody's surprise, chose war.

All this I watched unfold from afar, knowing its course and saying nothing. Occasionally Hannibal would look at me curiously, as if expecting some comment or reaction from me, but I would just smile and look away. Once he asked me why I had nothing to say, given my more outspoken comments when we met. All I could do was reply, "History is unfolding as it will, husband, and now is not the time for my counsel."

But now, watching Hannibal's elephants, and knowing his plans though he has not yet chosen to reveal them to me, I feel the time has come.

I have been thinking about this for a long time. I do not say I accept or believe what has happened to me, despite all the days when I have awakened into the same dream. I still feel that if I dare to call it real, then my last hold on the truth will fail and insanity irrevocably claim me. Perhaps such refusal even while I live under its sway is its own form of madness. But as I have wondered before when these thoughts have tormented me: what can I do, but act as if it is real? Stop acting and die?

So if I am here, is there a reason for it? I do not believe in fate. What would be the point? If our lives are ruled by fate, then there is no choice and no purpose to a pretense of choice. Even if we choose to do nothing but to drift with circumstances, that would also have been our fate. Then we might envy those who were fated to eat, drink and be merry for tomorrow they die, and pity those who were fated to build, create and achieve, at what cost to themselves? If we all float down the river of fate, we can only hope that the tributary it carries us through is a pleasant one. But is not such hope itself a form of choice?

If I do not believe in fate then I must believe in choice; and with choice, perhaps comes a second chance. Until now I have been cautious. History is uncertain, the words recorded on paper and stone just as prone to rumor, error and distortion as any other of the words of men. So I have tried to stay within the range of what might have been, given what is known. Nobody can walk through history without leaving some wake. But even my largest achievement to date, my marriage to Hannibal, is close enough to what was recorded that I think it will pass. If our names are a bit different, such errors are common enough to pass.

But if I am here for a reason, and the reason is redemption, then I must choose to act. To throw my caution to the wind and change history. The thought chills me, for why do I think that history can be altered, and what arrogance must I have to think it can be altered by me? Perhaps all I will achieve by trying is my own erasure from history, my personal death in this strange world far removed from my own. I think of Hannibal: of his courage, his willingness to grasp for the prize no matter the risk; sure in his power to succeed, steeled by his willingness to die if he fails. What can I do, but match the man who made me his wife?

I have been thinking about what I heard at the party that began this: that Hannibal is doomed to fail, no matter what he does. And with his failure, the fall of Carthage and the Phoenician ideals it stands for, incomplete or flawed as they may be now, follows. Yet perhaps I can find a better way.

I seek Hannibal out, and stand humbly before him. He looks at me, amused at my pose, knowing it is a thin skin over my true intent.

"My lord Hannibal, may I offer counsel?"

His amusement sparks to his eyes. "It must be something especially dangerous, if you choose to ask my permission for once, wife."

I ignore the subtle emphasis he places on that last word.

"May I sit?"

He gestures permission, his amusement melding with curiosity.

"My lord, your predecessor Hasdrubal was a brave and wise man."

"It is so."

"In a few short years he consolidated Carthage's power here, and made peace with the Romans too. Yet now you plan war."

A dangerous glint enters his eyes but he says nothing, daring me to go on with no signposts from his words. I take a deep breath and make the plunge.

"My lord Hannibal, I counsel you to reconsider. Leave Rome alone. Crush their armies here and they will accept peace. Then continue to build Carthage's strength in the west and south until Rome can be overwhelmed. Not now. If you take the fight to Rome now, all will be lost."

A familiar look enters Hannibal's eyes. Not the cool chess master, but the man of two and a quarter millennia ago, the man raised not only to command men but in a world where men ruled over women, especially in matters of war. What I see in his eyes now I have seen before: a battle between his cultural reflexes and his awe of me. I have an advantage in this fight in that Phoenician women were more equal than in many other cultures of the time. But this is Hannibal, master of men, and the advantage is slight. He has always won this battle before, controlling his anger and coolly assessing my words. I pray he will win it again, for I fear what will happen if he fails, what will happen to me if he loses his awe of me, what will happen to me if I lose his protection.

But I have to risk it. If Hannibal cannot win in war, the only solution I can see is for his people to avoid war, and grow their own strength while containing Rome. And I think they can do it. They have already spread across the Mediterranean. Surely they can go further around Africa; up north along the coast of Europe and to Britain. Left alone, Rome will conquer the Gauls, pushing up through their country from Italy, then eventually, over the channel to Britain. But Carthage can beat them to it. They can do what Hasdrubal did in Spain, and spread their influence by treaty and judicious warfare, growing inward from the waters and the coast. Rome will be constrained in the east by other empires as mighty in their own lands. If Carthage can contain them by controlling the west, Rome's power will be diminished while Carthage's is enhanced. Then, perhaps, Rome can be tamed, or if it will not be tamed, then one day crushed by a greater power.

That is what I hoped to achieve. But this time I have taken a step too far, and I see the moment when the battle in Hannibal's eyes ends in a blaze of fury.

"Enough!" he shouts. "You know nothing of war! Your counsel is the way of timidity! Of *cowards!* Do you think me a fool, to attack Rome ill prepared? You speak of Hasdrubal? You fool! This was his plan! Of course we know we must build our strength first! But we have done so, and now is the time to strike, to blunt Rome's point before it grows too strong!"

"My lord, I did not mean…"

"ENOUGH! Silence! Get out!"

I have seen Hannibal angry before. But never this angry at me. I quail inside, seeing the abyss yawning at my feet, and flee his presence.

~~~

It is late now, some hours after my disastrous meeting with Hannibal, and I seek him out; hoping to mend the bridge between us; fearing the future for both of us if it is too late. Not wishing either of us to sleep while this thing lies between us, lest it grow and consume us both.

He looks up at me as I enter but says nothing. At least his expression is one of weary curiosity, not contempt or hatred. But is it because he has regained himself, or instead lost that which that can never be revived? I do not know what to do, and I prostrate myself on the floor before him, my forehead resting on his feet.

"Forgive me, husband," I say nervously, "I did not mean to offend. I especially did not mean to imply you are a coward. I know that is far from the truth."

He says nothing, and I sit back to look up into his face. He turns his expression into a glare immune to my tears, a glower which pins me to the spot for a minute before his eyes soften. A little.

"For all the strange things you know, you do not understand war, my wife," he finally replies. "And as much as none who know you would call you a woman of humility, you are one of honor, so let me explain. I know what you sought to achieve. To let Rome sleep, while we build our power elsewhere. But Rome is not so easily ignored. It is like a great lion that can never be content. It might rest for a while, and appear peaceful. But it is consumed by a burning hunger, and soon enough it will rouse itself and rampage across the land until it has devoured its fill. There is no limit to its hunger, it wants the whole world, and there is no time for your plan to bear fruit. We will have spread ourselves more thinly, and not yet reaped our harvest, by the time Rome decides it must have us."

I nod my head. Not merely to appease him, but because his words ring true.

"Do you not know that Hasdrubal knew this, that I knew this? That Hasdrubal's peace would not last? Saguntum was just the first sign of their restless ambition, a cat cautiously poking its paw at an unfamiliar animal to test its ferocity. Do you think I took it in order to start a war we are not ready for? No. If I had not taken it, Rome would have gone further, escalating their provocations, with each one we turned aside from increasing their strength and boldness at the expense of ours. We knew war would come. It was always our plan to be ready for it, and to strike at the heart of Rome before it became too strong.

"But I do not plan to conquer Rome. Perhaps I could, but you are right to think it would be difficult on their home soil while our own army is far from home, with uncertain lines of support. But I do not need to conquer Rome. I can defeat their armies, sway their allies: and even Rome will see sense, and come to a peace more lasting and more favorable to Carthage than now. That is the way of war. It is not a fight to the death like two criminals forced to fight in an arena, where neither can afford to give quarter. Rather it is like a pair of stags fighting for dominance, who will battle until the stronger is known and then withdraw before one must die at great risk to both."

I look at him, tears still glistening my eyes, willing them not to fall. For he is wrong about Rome, and that is why he will lose. They will fight to the death rather than surrender, and in their own land they are too strong to kill, too powerful to subdue. But I cannot tell him this. He knows his way of war, and would not believe the Romans think it weak. If I try to tell him the truth, our own fragile peace will shatter, perhaps never to be repaired. Then all will be lost, for me, for him, for the dream of Carthage.

So I merely whisper, "I understand, my lord Hannibal. I will follow you wherever you go, and help you however I can. But the time may come when to do that I must offer you counsel again: only then it will be to do more than you would, not less. Will you give me permission to do that much?"

"I would not forbid your counsel, even if I could. But I cannot promise my listening will not come with anger."

"As long as your anger is not so hot that it consumes the... love... you hold for me."

"Did I ever..." he begins, and I hear the thought, "say I loved you?" But he stops, and simply says, "That I swear."

I feel confused, by my own question as much as his answer. But I hold out my hand to him, and allow him to raise me gently to my feet.

"Then come, husband. Let us quench today's flames in a different kind of fire."

Yet as we walk to our bed, I wonder what advice I might be able give him and whether any advice I offer can achieve any more than I did today.

~~~

She sleeps beside me, this strange woman I made my wife. I look at the faint smile on her lips, as if the pleasure of our recent union remains with her in her dreams.

The riddle of her nature still eludes me. Her words today enraged me, yet they are part of her nature, a part that curiously adds to her attraction. She is like no other woman I know, like few other men. She is no respecter of persons, not even me, speaking her mind in a manner that expects to be heard and valued. Yet oddly, this seems to reflect a greater and more authentic respect than those who accept my words because of who I am: as if speaking to another as her equal raises them up rather than pushing them down. Certainly I have observed that she does not deign to argue with those she has no respect for, turning away as if she does not see them. It is as if her great pride in her own mind extends to all with whom she chooses to share it.

Yet that is only part of her mystery. I remember her eyes on our wedding night. They were the eyes of someone who sees a hero and is proud to be accepted into his life. Yet what had I done to earn that look? I am a proud man, but I know that for all my pride in my abilities, and all the victories I have won, I have yet to earn the full measure of that pride. Yet she looked at me as if I had already earned it; and earned it doubly. But when I have achieved things, when I became leader in Iberia and built up victory upon victory, she was happy in my victories but the pride in her eyes was shaded with something else. As if her pride was somehow second-hand: the pride not in some new achievement, but merely the confirmation of something long past. It is as if I have a great future yet to be lived, and it is that greatness she sees: and she is content to be with me, watching as it unfolds but surprised by none of it. As if the hero she saw was not being added to by each new victory, but merely becoming complete.

I gently stroke her cheek with my fingers, knowing it will not wake her. No answers to the questions in my mind come from her sleeping form. But I know no more answers would come were she awake.

CHAPTER 14: THE ALPS

I had feared that Hannibal would not allow me to accompany him and his army on their march to Italy. I had feared that he would.

To his spirit of reckless challenge to gods, fates and conventions, to which I already owed my marriage and I suspect my life itself, I now owed this dangerous and uncomfortable journey as well. He did not ask my reasons and did not tell me his. But I had the feeling that he thought of me as a piece in a game as deadly as I was mystifying; that he did not know how I might be useful or to whom I was a danger, but he wanted me close regardless.

It has been a long journey, out of Iberia, across the Pyrenees and across the bottom of Gaul; sometimes fighting our way through or past hostile tribes, sometimes gaining their favor; facing or evading battle as circumstances demanded. There have been no major battles, but still Hannibal has displayed his superlative talent for tactics and bloodshed.

I have played no active part in these engagements. However I have tried to be seen at a distance, attired in my purple regalia, watching events unfold with a manner of haughty prescience. Rumors ripple out from my austere presence at Hannibal's side: goddess, priestess, Amazon, witch.

Perhaps with Hasdrubal's death the Romans thought his replacement would need more time to consolidate his plans and power, and were taken by surprise by the vigor of Hannibal's prosecution of the war. Their allies outside Italy could not stop a man like Hannibal. Their own force they sent to meet us was too late; Hannibal did not bother to face them, evading them by turning inland up the Rhone valley.

Now here we are in a peaceful river valley, the fatal peaks of the Alps rising before us. I gaze at our three dozen war elephants in the sad knowledge that many will not survive the coming trek; that even if they survive the Alps, few will survive the year. I gaze at our army, tens of thousands of men, with the same sad knowledge. Will I survive myself? History, for obvious reasons, is silent on my fate. I turn again towards the Alps and shiver, the cold peaks chilling my soul even before they can touch my body.

Tonight we camp. Tomorrow we face the mountains. As we eat our meal Hannibal glances at me, though I cannot tell whether it is amusement or merely reflected flames that play in his eyes.

"The way ahead is dangerous, my wife."

"As was the way behind, my husband."

"Yet you have offered no counsel."

"You have not needed any."

"Do you know what the coming days will bring?"

"Yes. We cross the Alps."

"Will we survive?"

"You already know many will die, of men and beasts."

"I know it. It is the way of war. Have you any wisdom for me?"

"You are wise enough for all of us. The time for counsel will come, but it is not yet."

~~~

Hannibal's crossing of the Alps is the stuff of legend as much as history. It is as bold and glorious and terrible and insane as one can imagine. It is a journey of grim determination and cold hard labor punctuated by terror. I think the screams of men and elephants will haunt my dreams forever. Still we drive on: for what else can we do? The goal lies forward, whatever the costs behind and those still to pay.

Occasionally I walk off to climb alone onto a high stone, my face raised toward the heavens; or I stand silently watching the army pass beneath my feet. The wind is like ice as it whips my gown around my body. No mortal could stand it long if they were wrapped in normal cloth, and even I have to be careful to protect my extremities. But men see, and wonder, and their whispers add to my legend.

Amid all the tales of Hannibal's crossing, one story stands out in famous uncertainty: the breaking of the rockfall. I cannot tell you the precise route we took over those stark mountains: one rocky path looks the same as any other to my untrained eye. But I can tell you that the tale of the rockfall is true.

We were trudging along the rocky path, heads bowed into a freezing wind carrying the curses and calls of men and animals. A loud cry of consternation came from ahead and a soldier rushed down the path toward us.

"My lord Hannibal!" he cried. "The path! The way ahead is blocked!"

We hurried up to view the disaster. A huge boulder had plunged into the narrow defile that our path wound through. Perhaps an agile man could climb over it; perhaps a small man could squeeze through a gap. But no army could pass it, and neither man nor elephant could move it from its seat. If it was weight alone, perhaps. But the boulder has driven hard into its resting place and is jammed tight.

That did not stop us from trying, but it proved as futile as it looked.

Hannibal is not fazed. After standing back observing his enemy, hands on hips as if declaring his distaste that some insensate piece of stone would dare oppose him, he issues his orders. Before long a blazing fire is lit at the base and sides of the boulder, and a line of men feed it with more fuel, like ants carting their booty to the nest.

A few times I notice Hannibal glancing at me curiously and I wonder how I have puzzled him this time. When the process is under way and we now just wait, he walks up beside me as I gaze into the inferno from a safe distance.

"Did you know this would greet us?" he asks.

I glance at him, startled. "Why do you say that?"

His perceptive eyes disturb me, and I turn away to resume my contemplation of the flames.

"When it happened you showed no surprise. No worry. Not even anger. You just watched, as if nothing I did surprised you. Not even my imagining I can burn stone."

"What difference would it make, whether I knew or not?"

"There is no way you could have known."

"Then there is your answer."

"You are a woman wrapped in mystery."

"You knew that when you married me."

"I did. And I am proud that I made you my wife."

I spin to face him, surprised. He rarely speaks of any tender feelings for me. That does not worry me, for I know ours is a marriage of convenience. If I feel uncomfortable that I am a pawn in his world-spanning games, I take comfort that it has kept me alive; and in the thought that perhaps he is the pawn in mine. I do not know what to say, but realize the truth the moment it escapes from my lips.

"No more proud than I to be your wife."

He smiles at me, almost tenderly. Then his eyes glint with amusement, as they so often do in my presence. "Yet you knew this would happen, wife, and did not tell me. Even when I told you I imagine I can burn stone, it passed by you without pause or comment."

At other times his accusations might have made me fearful. But there is something about his manner that tells me there is no danger in them this time. Whatever he suspects he has already accepted.

So for my response I glare at him, but it bounces harmlessly off the glint in his eyes. Annoyed, I put my glare into words.

"Even if I knew, what would have been gained by telling you? You would ignore me, or order me not to meddle in the affairs of the great Hannibal son of Hamilcar, who knows all things!"

To my surprise, the glint in his eyes takes on a new shade, not one of anger but one looking almost like hurt. He is determined to confuse me today.

"Or perhaps I know that you are as equal to this challenge as you have been to all others, and we shall march on through regardless," I add softly.

He smiles, somewhat more broadly now, and we turn to watch the blaze in silence.

~~~

Finally the flames are dying down, and Hannibal raises his arm in signal. Vinegar and water are released to pour onto the rock, exploding into steam; somewhere beneath the sound of its fury lurks a deeper, sharper cracking sound.

Yet whatever internal agonies our obstacle suffers, its groans are the only sign it gives us, and still it stands blocking our way, like a warrior bowed but still determined to hold the pass. But Hannibal knows his foe is weakened; encouraged, he signals his men to repeat the performance.

"How do you know this will work?" I ask him as we retire for refreshments.

"Men have been traveling mountain passes for a long time," he explains, "and we are not the first who have needed to break through rockfalls. This type of stone is known to be prone to cracking. How do you think it came to fall in the first place, if not by cracking off from its mother stone? Men have also noticed that vinegar attacks it, or it attacks the vinegar, producing bubbles where the two meet. That must both weaken it and add to the force on the rock caused by water turning to steam. The rock will fail, and we shall pass."

~~~

So now we stand before the rock again as the flames die, and watch as more vinegar and water is poured upon its fevered form. Again there is the explosion of steam; again there is the sound of its hidden wounds; but this time, there is a louder crack, and the rock splits into pieces. One large fragment teeters for long moments before falling to the ground with a crash. The boulder's fate is greeted by cheers, and men and elephants set themselves to the task of dragging the pieces out of the way and pushing them off the side of the mountain.

Then we resume our march across the Alps.

CHAPTER 15: TICINUS

S hall I tell you what it is like to cross the Alps with tens of thousands of men, dozens of elephants, and all it takes to support such a host? I think the project managers from my time would take one look at its immensity and flee whimpering into a more relaxing occupation, perhaps tea blending.

Somehow Hannibal did it, but his losses were horrific. The Alps are not forgiving in terrain or climate and many fell, too often literally. All told we lost several elephants, many of our supplies and nearly a quarter of our men; those who lived were exhausted, emaciated and many ill by the time we made our way down into the gentler embrace of the Po valley.

I cannot fault the Romans for expecting to fight their battles beyond Italy, never imagining that Hannibal would bring the fight to their own land by crossing the Alps. Who would anticipate such madness?

And now fewer than 25,000 of us stand on the home ground of one of the most successful militaristic cultures in history. If I did not know better, I would think we are all about to die.

As far north as this, at the very feet of the mountains, Rome's reach is at its farthest and weakest. Yet still the northern tribes who inhabit this region are no friends of ours. They do not attack us, however, perhaps because they are too busy with their own intertribal conflicts, or perhaps because even weakened as we are we are not a force to be despised. Surely they know of our presence, but they merely wait and watch with wary hostility.

We are now recovered enough to embark on the next stage of our campaign. Hannibal first tried an olive branch, offering a formal alliance to the Taurini, a Celtic tribe living in the upper Po valley. But whether out of fear of Rome (for it was surely not love) or antipathy toward Carthage, they refused.

It was a costly decision. For today I stand on a low hill overlooking their main settlement, now a smoking ruin, the town levelled and its people executed as a lesson to others that like Rome, Carthage will offer peace but answer refusal with fire and blood.

I have seen much brutality since my arrival in this time, but still I cannot watch it with equanimity. Yet I cannot bring myself to condemn Hannibal or his army for this act of terror. I understand that a small army, alone in a hostile country, cannot afford to show weakness, nor allow enemies to fester at its rear. I understand history. I know that however brutal our response to these people, it is little different from how they treat each other; no different from how the Romans treat everyone in their path. I take the long view. If Hannibal can succeed, perhaps the history of the world will take a different road: a path of peace and trade, not war, conquest and empire. That in the ledger of pain and glory over the centuries to come, whatever price is paid for its start will be more than balanced by prices not to be paid in the future.

So I tell myself. Yet my tears tell me otherwise, as I gaze upon the devastation and wish I was back studying history not living it.

~~~

Hannibal's crushing of the Taurini had its intended effect, and we now have a nominal alliance with the local Gauls. The might of faraway Rome cannot compete with the threat of our army on their doorstep, not now that we have shown our power and resolve.

However stealth is now not an option. Such a massacre cannot fail to reach the ears of Rome. Even so, Hannibal is surprised when he discovers that a Roman army is already nearby. Their commander, Publius Cornelius Scipio, having failed to meet Hannibal outside of Italy, has brought his men back to Italy to intercept him, though Scipio is even more surprised that Hannibal is already here.

Hannibal is not going to wait for the Romans to increase their strength. Scipio knows he is not going to wait. So the two come looking for each other with a fast-moving portion of their troops, Hannibal taking most of his surviving cavalry for the task.

And now the two armies have found each other, and we prepare for battle. I wonder what I should do.

The name Scipio is famous, but this is not the Scipio who one day will defeat Hannibal, it is his father. However I know that his son is with him. I also know that the elder Scipio almost dies in the upcoming battle when he is cut off with few defenders, and that his son will bravely rescue him. The younger Scipio is still a youth, a teenager (how innocently inadequate that term seems in the context of such violence!), unblooded. His actions today will set him on the path that ends at the end of Carthage.

How easy it would be to have father and son killed in the fray. I remember my earlier, nearly disastrous attempt to change history: to stop Hannibal's invasion in the first place. Hannibal and the Scipios have their place in history. Whatever place I might have had as Hannibal's Spanish wife, there is no record of me in the war. As I have feared before, perhaps all that will happen if I try to change history is that the attempt will remove my irritating presence permanently. But should I dare? Should I dare, and see the younger Scipio, one day to be named Africanus, slain today: never to become the man who defeated Hannibal?

It is not fear of my own death that stops me, though fear plays its part. It is the thought that stopping Scipio might achieve nothing. By the time he conceived his master stroke of forcing Hannibal out of Italy to defend Carthage, Hannibal had already spent years of a futile war in Italy, his chances of victory ever diminishing. Had Scipio not lured Hannibal back to Carthage, it is likely that eventually Rome would have crushed the dwindling remnants of his army anyway.

So I say nothing, and watch as by the banks of the Ticinus River Hannibal's cavalry envelops the Romans, breaks them into groups and routs them. The Romans lose over two thousand men this day, more than a fifth of their number. The Scipios are not among the dead.

CHAPTER 16: TREBIA

My enemy Scipio is no fool. Having lost the battle and almost his life, he did not lie around waiting for us to finish the job. I could not press my victory over his mobile force that day, for my own was far outnumbered by the Roman infantry back in their fort. We made haste, but Scipio had anticipated us and knew the danger of being trapped. By the time our army arrived the Romans had gone.

So the chase began. As I expected, with the arrival of a force able to challenge the Romans the Gauls are sensing blood and becoming restless. Over two thousand Gauls in the Roman camp betrayed their comrades, took the heads of their unfortunate neighbors, and defected with their trophies to our army. We received them as heroes, and I sent them away to encourage more Gauls to join our cause. But before we could attack, Scipio fled again, finally reaching a more defensible location. There, in the hills above the river Trebia which flows into the Po, they have constructed fortifications, are protected from behind and there is no suitable land for an attack. Now safe, they await the arrival of legions of reinforcements with which they hope to overwhelm us.

We have our own reinforcements. After our defeat of the Romans, our previously reluctant allies have acquired enthusiasm, and we now have their full support. Our army has already swollen by many thousands of men and we are camped in the plain below, waiting.

~~~

A white Christmas. How peaceful and good willed it sounds. But there will be no Christmases for centuries; if the Roman Empire never comes to be, perhaps there will never be any Christmases. Tomorrow is the winter solstice, and it is snowing. But there is certainly no peace or good will here tonight.

We are outnumbered, but not disastrously; perhaps against our thirty thousand the Romans have over forty. But as usual Hannibal knows how to lever every advantage into a greater one. The Roman camps are not united, and Scipio is still recovering from the wounds he suffered at Ticinus. The other commander, Sempronius, is nowhere near the strategist Scipio is. His dreams of glory coupled with his rashness will be his downfall.

It is Christmas Eve, and Hannibal is preparing his gifts.

~~~

My men are fed and greased with fat against the cold. Other men are hidden in ambush. My Numidian cavalry have crossed the river and are taunting the Romans, especially that fool Sempronius.

If Scipio were in command this would be wasted effort. No doubt he has been counselling restraint and to use the winter to rest and train their men. But the Roman force is divided by two consuls, who preserve their pride by alternating the command, and now it is Sempronius' turn. His rashness is exceeded only by his inexperience in military matters. So he does exactly what I expected, sending his as yet unfed army across the freezing waters in pursuit of my Numidians.

Those Numidians are as tough as they are prepared, and easily cross the river unscathed. But by the time the unready Romans have waded through the freezing waters and drawn themselves into ranks on our side of the river, they are sodden and shivering. They exceed us in number, but they are facing fighters who are warm, rested, and not hungry. Between that, our slingers and my remaining elephants, they are hard pressed, and when my brother Mago and his ambush force emerge from their gully to attack from the rear, they are routed.

~~~

I stand on a nearby wooded hill, far enough away from the battle to be safe, close enough to observe. My faithful Barekbaal and his small squad guard me, unwilling to leave me completely defenseless amidst the uncertain vagaries of battle.

And so I stand, and watch men die.

How many are there? This is just one battle in so many that have punctuated human history since before history began. And who can count the men whose youth and strength lie buried in the mud of the blood-strewn battlefields of history? But for all its horror, something else stirs within me to be a witness of one of the most seminal battles of history. Not Hannibal's first victory, nor even his greatest—if one measures greatness by slaughter, which is the only way to measure war—but the first major victory over the Romans by one of the greatest military strategists in history.

Hannibal's allies are more than Numidians, Celts and his Balearic slingers, whose deadly accurate stones have struck down so many today; they are more than his elephants. He has drawn into his quiver the freezing cold of the season, the deadlier cold of the river, even the hotheaded folly of his opponent. If there is anything he can use against his enemies, Hannibal will find it and bend it to his purpose, even if it is his enemies themselves.

Fifteen thousand Romans will die here today, a similar number captured alive.

But this is just a taste of what will come.

CHAPTER 17: CRITONIUS

How many of my men still live?

Somehow the Carthaginian dogs have defeated our army. It is not my place to blame my commander, though his rashness was surely part of our downfall. My own maniple was cut off and decimated; after fierce fighting I and a handful of my men broke free. We could do nothing but flee and hope to join up with a larger group; to retreat or fight some more I cannot yet say. Perhaps we will meet other refugees from our maniple. I hope so, but however many of us live or die the battle is lost.

We stumble into a clearing. What I see chills me to my bones. A woman stands nearby, her gaze fixed on her view of the battle's end as hair the color of dried blood whips around her face.

Despite the cold she is dressed only in a filmy gown of the richest purple, and the sight is so unexpected that for a moment I imagine this is all a dream.

Then I know what she is.

"Hannibal's witch!" I cry.

Time seems to slow. Startled, the woman's gaze turns toward us, as do the faces of her guards. We are badly outnumbered and cannot win. But we can strike a blow for Rome; and if the witch falls, maybe in the confusion some of us may escape. Even if we do not, we die in glory.

I signal my men, and feel pride at how quickly and unreservedly they form into a spearhead, myself positioned behind its point, and rush towards the woman. Her guards snarl and run to intercept us, but I know they will be too late. They engage my men, but our wedge breaks through their scattered ranks, the tip of our formation peels apart, and like an arrow from a bow I charge at the witch.

I see the look of shock on her strange face and expect her to turn and flee, knowing it will not help her: I am already bearing down on her, and before she can take more than a few steps I will be upon her and easily cut her down.

But she surprises me. Though unarmed, she crouches into an odd stance, facing me with arms wide as if embracing death. I am happy to oblige her and thrust my sword into her stomach: but she is no longer there! With the speed of a snake, somehow she has twisted her body to evade my stroke. But I am a Roman soldier, and my training is equal to her tricks. I twist my own body and arms, changing direction mid thrust and slashing my blade into her side and down toward her groin. Yet still she has the strength to grab my arm as she twists her body beneath me, and somehow I find myself in the air for a moment before crashing down onto my back! The breath is driven from my body, and as I lie there struggling to recover, the woman spins and stamps her foot hard on my wrist. My sword falls from my paralyzed hand, and before I can react she has scooped it up and holds it at my throat, driving it in deep enough for the point to draw blood, and I know I am about to die.

I lie here in shock, still struggling to force breath into my chest, wondering how I come to be lying helpless on my back when it should be her lying dead on the ground; my gaze darting between the sky above and her wounded side. I expect to see her organs spilling to the ground and her lifeblood spurting after them as she collapses. Yet she stands there, intact and unharmed. I have time only to wonder why she delays my own death.

Then I see her guards running toward us. My men are gone; dead or captured. The lead guard has a look of murder in his eyes and I watch him come, prepared to die as a Roman. But the woman holds up her hand and says something in their foreign tongue. The guards stop, their swords still pointed in my direction but their violence stayed for now.

My eyes keep returning to her side, which should bear a mortal wound yet is untouched except for the mark of my sword on its cloth; my mind can grasp neither that nor how I ended up helpless on my back, bested like a child by an unarmed woman. Finally able to breathe, I gasp, "You *are* a witch!"

She stares at me and I wonder if she can understand me. Then she speaks again to her men. I wince as heavy feet stamp on my arms, then two more swords press at my throat. Now she withdraws my sword, steps back and briefly regards me with her unholy eyes, the color of the sky. Giving me a dire look, she slides my own sword up between my legs and I fear she intends to castrate me here and now; but at the last moment she stops. She stares at me silently, but her message is clear: my life and future are in her hands, and anything left to me is at her choice and mercy.

If her purpose is to concentrate my mind on her and her words, she has succeeded admirably.

"I am no witch, tribune," she finally says in a low voice in my own language, accented but comprehensible. "If I were a witch, I would remove the useless parts of your manhood one by one, roast them over the fire and make you eat them!"

"With a nice chianti," she adds mysteriously. I do not know what this means or why she seems to find it amusing. I think I prefer never to find out what this 'chianti' is or what it might do to me.

"Then what are you? How do you still live? How did you toss me like a leaf onto the ground?"

"What I am is not your concern. You Romans think you should rule the world, yet it is far bigger than you can imagine and holds mysteries you cannot conceive of. Just know that the gods can be capricious and they can be cruel, but they can also be merciful. I leave you alive for a purpose. We have been enemies today, Roman, and may be again: but enemies can respect each other, can they not? Or is that also a concept beyond Roman understanding?"

"What purpose?" I ask, striking for the heart of the matter. "What price will you demand of me?"

"You have but to swear to do the task I set you, and you and your surviving men can go free and unharmed."

"I will never betray Rome, witch, not even for my life!"

"I do not ask you to betray Rome. I can see in your heart that you are an honorable man. For many men, honor is as cheap as their souls, do you not agree? But I would not ask a man such as you to dishonor himself."

I do not answer. How can those eyes penetrate even into my soul?

"What is your name, Tribune?"

I fear giving her my name, for what power might that give her over me? I know little of the ways of sorcerers. So I give her the name of a friend of mine who died in his youth; if even he is not beyond her power then we are all doomed.

"Publius Critonius."

She looks at me for a moment. "Truly you are a son of Rome, Publius Critonius," she replies with a faint smile. I do not know if this means I have fooled her, or not; and if not, whether her remark is a compliment or damnation.

"No, Publius Critonius, I will not ask you to betray Rome. I ask only that you help Rome. Take them my message. Tell your Senate what transpired here today. Tell them that the gods favor Hannibal. Tell them that the gods who favor Hannibal are merciful, and do not seek the destruction of Rome, merely its accord with the men of Carthage."

"Why should they believe you? Why should I?"

She shrugs, as if our belief or lack of it is of no moment. "You do not have to believe it. You merely have to report the truth and relay my words. You know what happened here. Rome thinks the whole world must bow before it. The truth is much greater than that, and the two of us are a symbol of it, Critonius. You thought I was easy prey, yet here I stand. Then you thought I would kill you, yet here you breathe. You feared I might take your manhood, yet I leave you your future. These are my words to you, and my only concern is that Rome hears them. What you say about them and what they do about them is not my concern."

She transfixes me with her gaze and adds darkly, "But understand, Roman. I do not care what you do about them, but your future and that of your people hinges upon it."

I look at her speculatively. I am willing to die; but not so stupid that I would die for nothing. "And that is all?" I ask, unable to keep the suspicion out of my voice.

"Swear by your manhood," she says, poking me there with the sword for emphasis, "by your honor and by your gods. Swear that you will carry the message I asked and that you will leave in peace, not attacking any person of Carthage until after you have returned to Rome. Then you and your men will be free to go."

I look at my sword, held in her hands. It would shame me to return to my family without it. "And my sword?" I ask.

"I will keep your sword, Roman, for I won it in battle, and not even equal battle. But you may take any other sword you choose from among your fallen comrades, to defend yourself on your journey."

My eyes wander: to my surviving men, to her miraculously intact body, to her burning blue eyes.

"Will… do you swear you will not force us to act against Rome?"

She laughs. "Courage as well as honor! I would not like to slay you, Critonius, but consider where your sword now lies: you are in no position to demand oaths from me. But I will tell you, as between people of honor: I ask only that you carry my message, and do not kill any more of my people while you do so."

I can die here; but would I then die honorably, or as a fool? Perhaps Rome is indeed better off knowing the things I have learned. If this woman wishes to control my mind and force me to betray Rome against my will, why would she go through this pretense of oaths and promises?

"Very well," I finally agree. "I swear to you before my men and the gods that I shall carry your message in peace to the Senate of Rome. This I swear by my manhood, my honor and the gods of my household and Rome."

She stares at me as if again looking into my soul, then nods to her men, who withdraw their swords from my throat but not from my direction. I rise cautiously and walk over to my men, who take the same oath.

Then I turn to her. "I have done as you have commanded."

She nods and turns to her men, again giving them instructions in their own language, before turning back to me.

"I have told them to escort you to the edge of the clearing and release you."

Then she adds in her implacable voice, "I have also told them that if you resist, tarry or return, to kill you all."

I look regretfully at my sword as I collect its replacement. I turn to her again: "But what of my fallen comrades?"

"We will treat them honorably. Go!"

We walk to the end of the clearing, half expecting treachery despite her words. But we are not molested when we reach the trees. When we are hidden from view but still able to see into the clearing, I stop and look back. She is still standing where I left her, looking in our direction as if she knows I am looking at her; holding my sword down at an angle like some avenging god or Fury. Then she turns on her heel and strides imperiously back into her tent, as if to underline not only that she knows I am watching, but that it is of no consequence to her.

I stand there for long moments, wondering what manner of creature this is. Then I signal to my men, and we vanish into the forest.

~~~

At last in the safety of my tent and away from the eyes of friends and enemies, I allow the sword to drop to the ground with a clatter and I collapse onto a stool. The dam of the tension holding me together now broken, I sit and sob into my hands, my whole body shaking.

Gingerly I feel my damaged side. I fear I have some cracked ribs, though they appear to remain unbroken, so my lungs are probably safe from jagged bone. Whatever the state of my ribs, the tenderness tells me I will be blessed with some spectacular bruises for a while yet. But the technological miracle of my gown has saved my life even if it has not saved me from pain.

My reflexes had not deserted me, but nor were they quite good enough. If I had ever thought that a Roman Tribune would be some effete aristocrat, this man has taught me better. But he was forced to overextend himself in his attack, thus granting me the momentum of his own strength. Then my body used its training in modern martial arts, honed over how many centuries, against him; and it was over before either of us knew it.

I expect Hannibal will be furious at me for letting them go, and I don't know how I can explain psychological warfare to him. But really, these people are like children, as superstitious in their beliefs as they are unrestrained in their emotions.

I hope I can rely on this man's honor. I told him I could see he was honorable: a safe enough claim, as how many men are not honorable in their own eyes? But will it be enough? And will it have any effect at all on the future?

I hope he will live to take my message to Rome. If I knew which God to pray to, I would pray I will also live long enough to find out whether he did.

CHAPTER 18: BAREKBAAL

When I was a boy, I met the noble Hamilcar, who blessed me with a smile and the words to my father that one day this lad would be a great warrior.

When I became a man, I was blessed to be accepted into the service of his son Hannibal. At the time Hannibal himself was just a youth, but we men could see in his visage the inheritance and promise of his father, and I saw in his eyes something even greater. And so I took my first steps on the road to the future Hamilcar had foretold for me.

Then I died.

But then I lived again, and I pledged my life to the woman whose hair was fire and whose eyes were sky, she who had dragged me from the depths of the sea and returned the breath to my cold dead body.

Truly I was blessed by the gods. I would have felt blessed if I were just another warrior in the army of Hannibal. Now I was that and more: pledged to defend the life of this woman some whispered was a goddess in human form and who was now Hannibal's wife. I knew some also whispered that she was a witch, or worse: but none dared utter such words in my presence, for my blade is as sharp as my arm is strong.

Such was my pride.

The pride of men amuses the gods. Often enough they let it be, finding amusement in watching them destroy themselves in their own time. Perhaps they decided I was too blessed and my pride no longer amusing. For then my pride came tumbling down with my vow, when a Roman came to kill my charge and I could not save her.

Fortunately she was somehow able to save herself, but though it may not be surprising that she who can breathe life into the dead can defeat a mortal man, it should not have been necessary. So my face still burns with my eternal shame when I recall the day.

Yet though I had failed her she did not condemn me. Instead she said she was glad that she had been forced to fight that man, for because of it she had made him her messenger to Rome: and who knew what good might come of it.

Hannibal was less understanding and I saw a dire fate glowing in his eyes, but she interceded on my behalf, saying there was nothing more I could have done than what I had and that she still had need of me. Perhaps to please her, perhaps because she was the unarmed woman who bested a Roman tribune coming to kill her with a sword, the rage in his eyes died and he agreed. I did not escape punishments, but those he meted out were less than I could have and willingly would have borne; less than I would have chosen for myself.

My lord Hannibal won a great victory that day, but then winter brought an end to our invasion. When spring came and we could move again, we knew the Romans would have been busy and have legions awaiting us in the places of their choosing.

There was a way to bypass the lurking Romans. But only a madman would have attempted bringing an army through the vast marshes at the mouth of the river Arno, dire swamps even worse this year due to heavier than normal flows. Even if it is the shortest route into the center of Italy, marching an army through it would require boldness bordering on insanity. However if the Romans thought Hannibal had exhausted his store of madness by crossing the Alps, they were mistaken.

Which is why he did it.

Now our army is slogging its way through this dread swamp. There are deaths of men and animals by drowning, by exhaustion, by simply being unable to go on and giving up in the mud. Still we push on, for what else can we do? However terrible the toll, we can neither stop nor return.

The march of the sun from morning to afternoon on this day is marked by the grim task of putting one foot in front of the other, step after step after tiring step through a swamp that neither wants us here nor is willing to let us go. As is my duty and habit I am accompanying Hannibal and my Lady. She is speaking to Hannibal when a puzzled frown crosses her face and she looks closely at him.

"Hannibal!" she cries, "Your eye is pink! It is diseased!"

"Is it? It does feel irritated, like there is sand in it. But it is nothing."

"It is not nothing, my husband. If we do not fix it, you will lose your eye!"

"It can wait until we reach drier land, where we can all rest."

"No, it cannot! Listen to me, my lord Hannibal! Surely I have proved myself to you. It does not matter how I know, all that matters is that I do know: and what I know is you will lose that eye if we do not treat it!"

He raises his eyebrow. "And assuming you know what cannot be known, how do you propose to cure it?"

My Lady pauses, as if her stock of arcane knowledge has suddenly run dry.

"I will have to think about it. Will you then allow me to treat you?"

"If you treat me, you will save my sight?"

"I don't know. I hope so."

"You hope so? If you know the future well enough to tell me I shall lose the eye, how can you not know the future enough to tell me you can save it?"

"I only know your fate if I do nothing. Once I act your fate is no longer fixed. Such lies beyond the power of even the gods to see."

Hannibal thinks for a while. "I suppose it can do no harm, and I would prefer to keep both my eyes. If you can find a treatment I will submit to it."

For some time we continue without further conversation, Hannibal scanning the route and his army, I alert for danger, she muttering strange incantations to herself in a tongue even stranger.

Whatever spell she was casting must be complete, for she looks at me and calls out, "Barekbaal!"

My heart swells, for surely this means she has truly forgiven my failure and wishes to entrust me with an important mission.

"I am at your service, My Lady."

She opens her mouth, but then looks sideways at Hannibal, before commanding, "Follow me!"

We move a short distance away then her piercing eyes engage mine, and I wonder what command she will issue. Then I know that she has not forgiven me, but has merely been waiting for an opportunity to show her contempt. For my mission makes no sense. It is to seek out honey and rotted bread, as if my only value from now on is to be a servant sent on meaningless errands. But if this is to be my punishment it is no more than I deserve.

And so I slog through even more mud, no longer trying to stay in a straight line to our destination, but trudging from beast to beast and man to man, the mud sucking at my toes like an unwanted lover unwilling to let me go. I have heard of the Greek Hades, and our people have similar tales. Perhaps she has sent me on this mission as a foretaste of my fate when finally I descend to the realm of the dead: eternally seeking the not-to-be-found, eternally dragging my exhausted body through a trackless mire on a mission never to be fulfilled.

I wonder if I should just stop, as too many have already done, and sink into the mire. But I cannot. Punishment or not, test or not, I cannot fail my Lady again, and so I force my lungs to breathe the tainted air and my legs to drag me through the tainted soil. And somehow I now find myself in possession of a small flagon of honey and a sack of green-furred bread. Those guiding the pack animals looked at me with dull curiosity but were too tired to express it in words and too uncaring to refuse me.

When I return to Angela with my prizes I expect her to send me on yet another futile mission. But there is no mockery in her eyes. Instead she thanks me with a smile and asks me to take the reins and guide her donkey. There she sits, lost in some world I cannot see, doing strange things with her bread and honey, singing a song under her breath in the language of the gods.

CHAPTER 19: ANGELA

I wake and when I look into Hannibal's eye, it is clear!
 I had started my new life in old Phoenicia filled with fear. The fear has never truly left me, but I admit I faced the prospect of travelling with Hannibal through the Alps into Italy with excitement as well. There are people in the world who would meet the opportunity to see some glory of nature such as a solar eclipse with blank indifference. So perhaps some people would find no excitement in the thought of living through one of the most dramatic military actions in history and seeing it with their own eyes. But no historian could contemplate it without feeling a thrill down to the bedrock of their being.

Trudging through a noxious swamp is far less romantic.

Then when I first saw the poisonous pink taking hold in Hannibal's eye, I recalled the tale that he lost an eye due to an infection he acquired somewhere on his journey through the Arno swamps.

Thus again I had to face my old quandary: *could I change history?* My earlier failure to dissuade Hannibal from even leaving Spain still haunted me and I considered its implications again. So far nothing I had done proved history was anything but immutable. Even my most dramatic achievement, my marriage to Hannibal, remained consistent with history as known in my time: not perfectly consistent, but close enough given the uncertainties in any history. Indeed, part of the art of the historian is comparing disparate records and trying to extract the truth from amongst their contradictions; or alternatively, deciding whether two tales in agreement are really mutually corroborating independent reports or simply copies, distortions and all.

It seems implacably logical that history, once it has happened, cannot be changed. As the great Persian poet Omar Khayyam wrote so hauntingly:

> The Moving Finger writes; and, having writ,
> Moves on: nor all thy Piety nor Wit
> Shall lure it back to cancel half a Line,
> Nor all thy Tears wash out a Word of it.

But if our understanding of history is elastic, could that be true of history itself? Perhaps it is like a rubber sheet stretched over a metal framework: the sheet can be distorted while the underlying structure remains unbent? Or maybe, just maybe, if we can apply force around the right fulcrum, could even the structure itself be warped?

Hannibal's losing an eye was a matter of history, to be sure. But it was more a decoration on the surface of the past rather than an essential part of its structure, for it does not appear to have directly affected the outcome of any battles. Yet unlike my marriage, preventing it would leave no doubt: unlike vague reports of his wife's name and paucity of details on her origin and whereabouts, the matter of his eye is definitive.

So it was not only my growing affection for Hannibal and my human desire to salve another's suffering which made my decision. I would push history and see how hard it pushed back. Failure would merely leave things as they were meant to be. But success... if I succeeded, who knows what else might be possible?

Once the hard part of persuading Hannibal was over, all I had left to do was find a cure in the middle of a swamp.

Antibiotics were one of the greatest advances in medical treatment of my age, so my mind turned to the first and most famous of them, penicillin. It is very effective against a lot of germs, so I thought there's a good chance it would cure conjunctivitis. I racked my brains for anything I could remember on the subject. I knew it was a natural product and it came from a fungus, that green mold you see on rotting bread and fruit. I thought I should be able to get some of that. One thing you can say for this ghastly era, finding rot and mold is not a problem.

But then what? I doubted I had time to brew some penicillin even if I could work out how: by the time I managed that his eye was likely to be irreparably damaged. Not to mention the other problems with my brilliant idea. How would I know that my green mold was the right species, and if it was that it was a strain that made penicillin? Visions came to me of epidemics of ergot poisoning in the Middle Ages… of madmen dancing down streets. Not everything produced by a fungus is good for you. If it were true that I could change history, I could just as easily make things worse rather than better. What if I sent him mad, or killed him? My own death would surely follow, and I shudder to imagine what his troops would do to the woman who killed Hannibal, in the protracted interval before finally allowing her to die.

Mulling these depressing thoughts, I decided I might as well find some moldy bread and hope to find inspiration in its uninspiring depths. It was the simple thought of food that brought the inspiration, and I hoped I wasn't asking too much of either our supply train or the gods. For I had recalled that honey is reputed to have antibiotic properties and the ancient Egyptians had used it to treat infections. Perhaps the two together would double my chances, and that any nastiness in the bread might be counteracted by the honey. I even decided to throw in a pinch of sulfur, which I vaguely recalled had medicinal properties. Fortunately there was no FDA in this era.

I am not a complete idiot. While Barekbaal sought my ingredients, I sought out what passed for a physician in the army. Perhaps Hannibal had lost his eye from a delay in treatment rather than lack of one. Yeah, right, Angela! I might as well have spun anticlockwise chanting as follow his advice.

Fortunately Barekbaal found what I needed. So muttering the magic incantation 'synergy' in the hope it might produce some, and trying to ignore the inconvenient thought that I had no idea what I was doing, I prepared my potion. I scraped the worst of the green powder off the bread, steeped the rest in honey thinned with a bit of wine, then squeezed out the liquid through some cloth. Surely, I thought, if this mold makes penicillin it does so to knock out competition for its food supply, so my nice ripe bread should already be infused with it: I admit I took liberties with the meaning of the word 'surely'. This concoction I brought to Hannibal, telling him it was a potion made with honey; somehow I neglected to mention all the other details of its manufacture. I slathered it in his eye and he bore it like a man, that is to say, muttering darkly.

Now we have left the swamp behind and our army is recovering in a gentler locale. Perhaps my optimism is premature, and his eye will take a turn for the worse. Or maybe the rubber sheet of history will find a way to snap back and take his eye by some other misadventure.

I know what I did was reckless, but I had decided this was a time for boldness. That is what I tell myself, though it is also possible that the dark mood induced by trudging through a swamp may have contributed to my rash attitude. I am tired of the blood, the filth, the fatigue and the fear, especially when all I have to look forward to is more of the same for fourteen long years, when my only escape will be to have those years cut short by a death likely to be as painful as it is inevitable.

I think about all the threads I have planted along my journey, with no clear plan of their destination, no real faith that they could have one.

Now against all odds I have lured the moving finger back at least this little bit, to cancel a word or two: and what might be written in its place?

And thus emboldened, or maybe merely catching madness from my husband, I begin to wonder what else I might do to history.

CHAPTER 20: LAKE TRASIMENE

We have recovered from our journey through the swamp. Most of our brave elephants survived the Alps, but between winter and the swamp a mere two elephants remain in our service, and our army is again somewhat depleted.

I do not like war, and I must continually tell myself not to judge earlier ages by the standards of our own. It is what they were born into, and how many of us who would condemn them can honestly say we would have done any differently in their place? How many of us have had the ability, let alone the courage or power, to choose some better morality, above that poured into our minds by parents and culture? And if we dare judge all men of an age by their worst actions, perhaps those earlier ages would themselves recoil in horror from us, were they to see what men did to each other in our own great World Wars.

My present discomfort stems from Hannibal's tactic of ravaging the countryside in order to not only supply his army but provoke the Romans into battle. It is one thing to kill armed warriors who are as ferociously trying to kill you, another for an army of thousands to pillage the helpless. But then I think again of our own World Wars and what both sides did to the civilians who got in their way. In any case it is war. Are the Carthaginians right to seek the subjugation of Rome? Are the Romans right to seek the destruction of Carthage? If so, at what level of strategic death and ruin does right become wrong? Hannibal is not looting the countryside because he takes pleasure in it. He is doing it to undermine loyalty to Rome, a distant power unable to protect them; he is doing it to enrage the Romans sent to do the protecting, and lure them into hasty battle. Such are the stratagems of war by an outnumbered force in the heartland of a powerful enemy.

Nor can I call myself innocent, as I feel sorrow and guilt even while knowing I shall continue to support Carthage in the hope of a better world. In the scales of my soul will that better world truly outweigh the carnage of the present? I remind myself that all this would have happened without me. Yet the reminder feels inadequate when I see the trails of smoke in the distance and the twisted bodies on the ground.

There are about to be a lot more of those. The latest Roman consul to come against us, Flaminius, has had enough and is pursuing us, partly from anger, partly because we have skipped around him and are now between him and Rome itself. Hannibal's army is arrayed near Lake Trasimene, waiting. Last night, campfires burned far in the distance, as if we are more distant than we are. Troops lie hidden in the trees. Nature aids us with a healthy dose of fog. The trap is set.

The trap is sprung. As soon as the Roman force clears the end of the valley in pursuit of our visible forces, formerly invisible forces descend on their rear. It is a massacre. Many of those not cut down by cavalry are forced into the lake, to drown or be trapped and slaughtered. As disasters go, it matches Trebia, with another fifteen thousand dead and a similar number taken prisoner.

If Flaminius learns the folly of impetuous arrogance compared to the wisdom of creative planning carried out with brilliant execution, it is a lesson as short as his remaining life.

I do not stay to witness the end of the battle. I don my regalia and signal Barekbaal to follow me to a small glade I had found. Then I turn and address him.

"Faithful Barekbaal! Our lord Hannibal has won another great victory. Now I must commune with the gods. Guard me. When Hannibal returns, tell him I request his attendance."

With that I sit on the ground, cushioned by greenery. I assume the lotus position and close my eyes. How much of this is theatre and how much an attempt to calm my racing heart I do not know. I hope it is more effective at the former than the latter. For now I will grasp the nettle, and on my decision my own fate, and perhaps the fate of world, may hang.

I do not know how long I sit like this. I do know it calms me. The clash of weapons and the cry of man and beast recede; the feel of wind and scent of vegetation come to the fore of my mind. I said I would commune with the gods and maybe it was the truth, for the wind and the trees speak to me, and tell me I do right. I hope they speak the truth.

At last I hear soft voices, and I attune my senses to my immediate surroundings. Soft footfalls and the jingling of metal announce a man's approach. It must be Hannibal, for there is no other Barekbaal would permit to approach. When he stops before me in silence I wait a few seconds then open my eyes.

It is time.

~~~

When I return to camp, a messenger tells me my wife wishes to speak with me. I find her sitting on the ground in a strange position, looking as if she might float up into the sky. Her rich purple robe flutters around her in the breeze; she has let her hair loose, and it too dances to the same inaudible tune. Her eyes are shut and I wonder if she is asleep, but she seems too erect, her body oddly relaxed yet taut for action.

I stand before her, wondering if she knows I am here, wondering if I should call her name. Her eyes flash wide open, their startling blue adding to the effect, but she does not smile. Instead she regards me gravely, then speaks in a low but steady voice.

"My lord Hannibal, you have won a great victory."

"I have."

"If you continue on your course, you will win an even greater one."

"That is my aim."

"If you continue on your course, you will lose the war."

I do not ask how she knows this. I simply ask, "How?"

"You do not understand the Romans."

"I understand them well enough to crush them in battle."

"That is your downfall. You think that crushing them in battle will defeat them."

"It is enough. Already their allies defect to our cause. You say a greater victory awaits me? If this battle is not enough to sway them, surely the next will be, and they will be moved to seek peace. In that peace we shall regain what we have lost, and more."

"No, my lord Hannibal."

"No?"

"No. You think of your battles as fights of honor, where the loser will know they face a superior foe and will seek peace in order to lose no more. That is not how the Romans think. You are a proud man, my lord Hannibal. The Romans are also proud, even more proud than you; with a pride that becomes arrogance. Their arrogance is matched only by their loyalty to their own republic and its destiny. Their arrogance will lead them into their greatest defeat ever. Understand me, my lord Hannibal. In their next battle they will not lose five thousand men; they will not lose fifteen thousand men; they will lose over forty thousand men at your hands."

If she seeks to dissuade me, she is choosing a strange path. I stare at her in silence.

Then her voice continues in its implacable lowness. "Yet still they will not surrender. They will vow to fight you to the end of their days. But they will not face you. They will harass you, they will avoid you, they will deny you. Few of their allies will turn to you; those who do will weaken you rather than strengthen you, for instead of adding to your army you must leave men behind to defend their cities. You will spend the next dozen of years in this country, until one day a general as good as you will take the war to the gates of Carthage itself, and you must go to their aid. No man can win all battles, my lord, and that is the one you will lose. It will be Carthage which begs for peace. Rome whose ascendancy is assured. And within the lifetime of men alive today, that ascendant Rome will bring the war to its ancient enemy for the last time, and Carthage will be destroyed forever."

I stare at her, aghast. I do not believe her. How can she know such things? Is she, after all, an agent of my enemies? A master strategist, fastening herself to my side for all these years, pretending friendship, sharing my bed, all the while patiently awaiting her chance to betray me? But something about her: her otherworldliness, her implacable certainty, the courage she must have to utter these words to me: something about her gives me pause. I stare at the ruin of my dreams, unable to deny the vision. Perhaps it is that which forces me to utter my next words.

"And me? What will become of me?" I whisper.

"You will fight the Romans to the end of your days, my lord, until one day, betrayed, you will take your own life."

"So that is why you tried to stop me…"

"That is why I tried to stop you. You hate the Romans, my lord. I do not judge your hate. But are the deaths of the thirty thousand enough? Are the deaths of the next fifty thousand enough? Will they slake your hate, even if all you do is pave the road to the death of Carthage with their bodies?"

"Then what should I do?"

"I do not know."

"You do not know? Then what is your purpose?"

"I do not know what can save you. But I do know the one thing which might."

"Will you...?"

She must have seen the fear and hunger in my eyes and known what I would ask, for she reached out and touched my hand.

"That is part of it. But not in the way you think. The way ahead is hard. So hard we must gamble all on one throw of the dice, and thus the gods will decide whether we live or die."

Then she closes her eyes, and breathes deeply, as if she cannot go on. And though she sits there as if resting, it seems as if she stands on the edge of a precipice looking down into a darkness whose end she cannot see, and she fears to take her next step.

Then she opens her eyes, and with the fear I see decision.

"Your next victory will be far from Rome. Though their army will be crushed, by the time you could reach Rome itself it will be too late. Their hate and fear and pride will have fused into a wall that cannot be breached. You think the legions of dead will dissuade them? They will already be replaced. But today you are close to Rome. When word of this battle reaches them, the tale of another disaster so soon after the last one, a disaster in the heart of their own country and so close to their city, they will be appalled. You must march on Rome as soon as your army is able to move. You must bring the war to their gates, while there is still time. You must chase the news with your army before their terror can abate."

"I have no siege engines capable of taking a city such as Rome."

"Build them."

"They will not surrender. And when their armies come we will be trapped between their legions and the walls we cannot breach."

"Perhaps. But it is our only chance. This is the time when they fear you the most. They teeter on the edge of surrender. You must strike at their heart now, push them over that edge, or you have lost Carthage."

Then she closes her eyes again, as if she has no more to say. I see a tenseness in her, as if she fears my only answer will be to plunge my sword into her heart, but she will accept even that.

I gaze at her, studying the mystery who is Angela, my wife. She is beautiful at this moment, as the slanting sunlight from the sinking sun strikes her hair and garment. I look at her body, the body I own and have loved; I try to see into her mind, a mind I have never owned or understood. Why did the gods send her to me? To test me, to torment me, to save me, or at this last moment to betray me?

I do not know. I look up to the sky but it does not speak. Whatever the gods want of me, they want me to decide it myself.

CHAPTER 21: ROME

Hannibal did not kill me that day.

He stood there for a long time, saying nothing, until finally he turned and walked softly away. For a while I wondered if men would come for me and I would die in this nameless field, spurned and forgotten. But none came, and as the chill deepened I again opened my eyes, rose and walked back to the camp. Hannibal greeted me as if nothing had happened. I feared that in his mind, nothing had.

But now we stand in sight of Rome. I gaze on it in wonder. This is the city which more than any other will shape the world, the start of an empire of glory and blood. Even now, in the days of the old Republic long before Caesar prepared the way for Empire, I feel I should bare my head in homage before it.

But I have come to destroy it.

~~~

I had a long talk with Hannibal. At some level he must love me, for he does not like my plan. I am sure that the chess master in his mind approves of it. Or maybe I fool myself, and what Hannibal disapproves of are the consequences of my failure when I am risking everything on one wild and dangerous play.

Now there is no more I can do than go forward. I hope I make an imposing sight. I ride Hannibal's favorite elephant Surus, the largest of only two survivors of the rigors of our journey. On one side of me strides Barekbaal, on the other a well-muscled warrior with dark, constantly shifting eyes. Both are armored and carry bow and arrows.

They can do little to protect me if the Romans mount a serious attack, but they are something, and a warning to any lone assassins that vengeance may be swift.

In the ancient world the lives of emissaries were usually respected, much like diplomats of my time and for similar reasons. In war you often want or need to talk, and if you kill the emissaries of your enemies you are likely to lose your own in like manner. Throughout history knowledge has been power, and the short term satisfaction of killing an ambassador is likely to backfire badly. Unfortunately the devil is in the word 'usually', and I recall a movie I watched wherein the Spartans kicked the Persian ambassador down a well to teach him a permanent lesson in subtle diplomacy. As Hannibal took pains to remind me, his recent victories have generated as much hatred as fear, and my personal reputation as a witch or worse is not going to endear me to our enemies.

I have wound my gown as tightly as I could around my body and as high to my neck as I could, but even if that can protect me from arrows it will not save me if I am hit in the head. Perhaps like the Saxon king Harold in centuries yet to unfold, an arrow in the eye will be the end of me.

Already I have changed history, and today I might learn how far I can alter it. In my time Hannibal never marched on Rome, not now, not even after his crushing victory at Cannae. But my image of the rubber sheet over an inflexible skeleton haunts me. Maybe I have already distorted that rubber sheet to its limit and it is about to snap back to its ordained course, casting me from it. If I die today, perhaps all that history will record is that Hannibal marched on Rome, the Romans spurned his overtures and threats, then history continued on its briefly detoured course, having discarded the inconsequential life that dared challenge it. Maybe he will even lose his eye here, expunging the last trace of my futile meddling.

Now my guards stop just out of arrow range, while I continue slowly forward. I must show the courage to face my enemy, to stand uncowed in the shadow of death. As an emissary I am unlikely to face a storm of arrows, but as a despised enemy I might face a few. So Surus carries me closer, to within the range where I could be hit but it would take a skilled or lucky archer to manage the feat.

There I stop. And there I address the Romans.

"I speak to the Senate and people of Rome! Who will listen?"

I see faces watching me and a susurrus of comment, but none reply.

"I speak to the Senate and people of Rome! Who will listen?"

"Here is your answer, witch!" a lone voice shouts, and a moment later I see six arrows arcing towards me. Much as I would like to face them serenely, I cannot stop myself crossing my arms across my face, hoping it looks like someone warding off evil rather than the truth: a girl whose heart pounds in the terror of expecting her end. Not surprisingly, most of the arrows fall short or wide, but one glances off my arm and then a moment later I double over at the hard punch of another striking me directly, low in the chest.

A mocking cheer begins from the ramparts, but it falters when I straighten and raise my head to stare at them. I pull the arrow from the folds of my gown, hold it high for all to see, then contemptuously cast it to the ground.

"I speak to the Senate and people of Rome! Who will listen?"

The tone of the muttering has changed and I sit and wait in fake serenity. I begin to see clumps of men in the whiter and colorfully striped garments of the patrician class, but despite the murmur of conversation that expresses fear, hate and excitement, none address me. I wait a while longer then speak again.

"Senate and people of Rome! You did not believe that Hannibal would face you in Italy! You did not believe that Hannibal could defeat your armies! You did not believe that Hannibal would reach your gates! Yet here we are! You have heard the tales, and trembled. Now you see with your own eyes. Do you doubt that the gods favor Hannibal?

"Do you think Rome is invincible? Has it not been sacked by others before us? Is that not why you now have these walls to hide behind? But whatever you have been told and whatever fears drive your nightmares, we are not barbarians seeking to sack your city, rape your wives and enslave your children! We seek only accord with Rome!"

I swallow to wet my dry throat, and wonder if my speech is over the top. If one can be over the top when playing for the future of the world.

I lower my voice, not so low they cannot hear me; low enough that they have to try.

"I know you hate us. Many among you wish we had never come to your land. Many of you curse the ground we stand upon, as if your curses could make the land swallow us into Hades. I understand, people of Rome. I understand the pain of those of you who have lost sons: brave men, fighting for Rome! For we honor all men of courage and honor, even our enemies!"

I move my head, scanning the listeners on the walls. They watch back, silent. Then I raise my voice again.

"I do not ask you to fear us! I do not ask you to love us! I merely ask that in years to come you will not look back in regret at this day, but in pride that you lived it. That you will not look back upon it in the pain of loss, the loss of sons and daughters and glory, and cry that you wish you had heeded wisdom not hate! That you look back in pride! The pride of men, who like Odysseus of legend knew when to pause in your anger and your hate, and choose the way of wisdom instead! It is easy to be afraid! It is even easier to be angry! All I ask of you, men of Rome, is this. You see before you a mere woman. Do you think I chose this fate? Do you think I wish to be here, alone, facing down the pride, bravery and might of Rome? When I could be living a life of peace and tranquility in the love of husband and children?

"No, I did not choose my fate! None of us choose our fate! But we choose what we do with it!

"Do you love war so much that you would refuse our peace? Do you love your sons so little that you would rather send them to die at our hands than to live to raise their own sons?"

Then, history forgive me, I channel Yasser Arafat. Sometimes you have to take inspiration where you find it.

With my right hand I draw Critonius' sword from where it hangs by my side, and brandish it high.

"I come to you with two hands, men of Rome! In one hand, I bring you war and death!"

Then I raise my left hand high holding an olive branch, and add, "But in the other I bring you peace, life… and if you have the courage to accept it, even friendship between our two great peoples!"

I lower my sword to point at Rome, but keep the olive branch high.

"Today I have come bearing an olive branch and a sword. Do not let the olive branch fall from my hand! I repeat: do not let the olive branch fall from my hand!"

I am silent for long moments as I sweep my eyes over the crowds watching me.

"So choose, people and Senate of Rome!"

And with that I turn Surus and we head back to our camp as if their choice is no longer my concern, their life or death equal in my eyes.

CHAPTER 22: NIGHT

There is no official reply from Rome.

But men come in the night. It is not that difficult to leave Rome, though I am sure it is dangerous enough. Rome must keep at least its supply lines to its port open or we could quickly starve them into submission.

These are not mere ruffians or cowards. Those who are not plainly slaves and bodyguards are patricians, with even some Senators among them. I do not partake of their conversations, merely sit in the shadows and watch in silence. Occasionally I see eyes flick in my direction. Some are curious, some filled with fear or awe or hate, some as if they wonder what it would be like to own my body. To them all I return a gaze not of contempt but of indifference, and all turn away.

They speak loudly of their loyalty to Rome, these men. Do they seek to convince us, or themselves? Not that I would wish them dissuaded. Do even I believe that what we seek is best for Rome? Perhaps it is. All those lives lost at Cannae will not be lost. Rome will be the poorer: but not because they produce less wealth, rather because they will steal less from the world. They will gain peace with Carthage, at least for a while: but will what the world gets in place of the famous Pax Romana, the Peace of Rome, be better or worse?

I must believe it will be better. I do believe it will be better. But I have no way of knowing. I can look only into the future as it has been. If we fail here, perhaps that will be the future and maybe it is the only future there ever could be. But if we succeed, the future becomes as opaque to me as it is to all people.

Whether or not these men believe they are saving Rome, they remain focused on their own interests and negotiate strongly for their positions, powers and privileges in the new order.

Then plans are laid for how to bring that new order into being.

CHAPTER 23: VALERIUS

Hannibal's army has reached Rome, but our walls and gates are strong and our city will never fall to them. His army is too small. So they can camp outside and spit insults and death at us, but they cannot even surround the whole city: not without risking a sally that would smash through their ranks then turn to crush them against the walls. If their siege grinds on, no doubt fewer merchants will arrive and even fewer leave, but for now the flow of trade continues, reduced no more by the storm of Hannibal than it is by more natural storms of wind and rain. Beyond an undercurrent of fear running through the city, life goes on as it did before the enemy came.

But Hannibal is cunning and we must be alert to trickery. So I and the guards beneath me are careful to inspect all who seek entry into Rome.

A large cart containing several barrels approaches, led by a man in the dress of Etruria, accompanied by four husky slaves.

"What is your business?"

"I bring trade goods to Rome," he replies in a foreign accent, though I expected that from his raiment.

"You braved the armies of Hannibal?"

He shrugs and spits onto the ground. "I did not expect to find them here! I had already set out on my journey, and now feel I would be safer in Rome than on the road waiting for his brigands to rob me."

While I engaged him in conversation, my men had quickly checked his cart and now they signal to me. There is nowhere for men to hide and they carry no military weapons.

"So what do you bring?"

"Mainly fine wine."

I tap on each barrel. Most resound in the way liquid does, but the largest is very strong and delivers a more muffled sound.

"And this one?"

"A luxury foodstuff."

"Open it."

He frowns, but when he opens his mouth to object he notes my hand resting not quite casually on the hilt of my sword, and I almost hear it snap shut. He contents himself with muttering to himself as he obeys, if not with good grace then with acceptable speed. When at last he removes the lid, I see the barrel is full of small black grains.

"What kind of food can this be?"

"It is a rare spice from far to the east. I am hoping to open up a market for it in Rome, for I know exotic tastes are much in demand here. Try it if you will."

He grabs a grain and puts it in his own mouth, crunching it between his teeth; so assured he is not trying to poison me I do the same. I frown and spit. It has a salty and bitter flavor, not at all to my liking.

"People eat this? It is awful!"

"Spices often are, on their own. Have you ever tasted pepper? This is a kind of pepper, not as sharp but with a pungency all its own. People do not eat pepper itself, they add it to enhance their dishes. You would be amazed at the transformations a talented cook can achieve."

I am dubious that he will make much money from his black spice, but nor can I see any danger in it. I wave him through and turn my attention to the next cart.

Chapter 24: Angela

Hannibal does not wish to besiege Rome for too long. He is well aware that while his army is camped by the city his mobility is compromised and his talents of deception and ambush crippled. Without a way to quickly breach its walls, it would never fall in the time he has available before legions from outside descend upon us and we are trapped and slaughtered.

The night after the men came to see us, flaming arrows and boulders were hurled at the city of Rome, and an army of Gauls came screaming at the gates but were repulsed.

The night after that and again after that the same thing happened, at different gates but with the same result.

And now tonight it is happening again. But the defenders do not know they have already lost. Or we have. This night will end it, one way or another.

When Hannibal told me his plan, I feared for him. "But my lord Hannibal," I said, "Are you sure you can trust these men? What if it is a trap?"

He gave me an ironic smile. "Of course it might be a trap, though looking into the eyes of those men I believe not. But did you not start this, Angela? Why then do you quiver at the sight of me seeking to finish it?"

"But you don't have to go! Your head is the greatest prize the Romans could seek! Let others take the risk! Why should it be you?"

"Do you really expect me to hide in my tent while others sally forth to set the course of history? Do you know me so little?"

He reached out and touched my hand.

"You know we have made three plans, and our Roman allies each know only their own parts, not those to be played by the others. And you of all people know that one plan is known only to us, and that is the one I await and will lead if it succeeds. We still might be rushing into a trap. If it is a trap or if the Romans rally well enough, or are even lucky enough, I might die. But that is the risk and fate all warriors face in every battle they join. It is a risk and fate I have embraced since my youth. And to defeat Rome is why I embraced it. Am I to turn away at the last moment, and lose it all?"

I bowed my head, knowing he was right. If I have bent history too far then he will die tonight and I will follow him soon enough. If the battle is lost I have instructed Barekbaal to end my life. Much as I fear baring my neck to his sword, it would be a more merciful end than what I would receive at the hands and other parts of the Romans when they catch me, as catch me they most certainly would. The mystique I have built around myself is as fragile as an eggshell and will protect me for as long; and the measure of my success in creating my mythos will be the measure of the brutality of Roman revenge when they discover how easily it is smashed. But Hannibal was right in more than that. I had set this course in motion and must have the courage to see it to its end. On such courage has all greatness in the world ever been built.

Yet my old pain persists. Men will die tonight. Guards at the gates, betrayed by their own people. Others destroyed by my own actions and dashed uncomprehending to their deaths. Men, women and children slain at the hands of Hannibal's howling army once it is unleashed inside the city, as its soldiers seek revenge for comrades slain, plunder to enrich themselves, or simple slaking of their cruelty and lust. Can I deny my guilt in the coming slaughter? If Rome falls tonight their disaster at Cannae will be averted. But do the lives that might save truly pay for the other innocent lives my actions will end? How does one measure it? Is there some cosmic scale upon which we can truly weigh the lives of some against the lives of others, and clean away the blood of one with the living breath of the other?

I do not know. I know only that Death follows in my wake, I who sought to make the world a better place. I pray that I am right.

And now the time has come.

Chapter 25: At The Gates

Sound roars in my ears. Or is it just the echo of my own blood howling its battle cry? Part of our army, greater in sound and fury than in numbers, bashes their shields and hurls invective at a distant gate, while flaming arrows arc overhead and bring fire, death and panic to the city. The Romans are not fools, but while they dare not leave the rest of their city undefended, even they cannot help but concentrate their forces near the threat. They suspect a trap. But is the trap the feint at the gate, or the previous nights when no attack materialized?

I, Maharbal, am Hannibal's most able and trusted commander, and mine is the honor to command. I lie in wait with my men in the darkness beyond another part of Rome's imposing wall. Then the signal comes. At yet another gate, an even fiercer howl arises with its accompaniment of fiery arrows. Our few ballistae, constructed at speed while we camped near Rome, now begin to batter the wall there, as a screaming mob descends upon it.

The signal is not for us. It is for the men inside, and we wait with the tension of men waiting for battle. Will our allies fail? Or will they betray us? The time is upon us, for the gate creaks open. We do not scream, but urge our horses forward as quietly as we can. We know other gates should open tonight, and if none do then our chances of fighting our way back out of the city are grim. But we do not dwell on this. We think only of the plan and our part in it, feel nothing but the power of our horses and the rhythm of their hooves, the rhythm of war.

We are in! Men with swords marred with dark liquid salute us as we pass, too quickly to be sure the liquid is blood and the shadows by the wall are bodies. As our cavalry storms through the gate into the heart of the enemy city, no alarm is raised, and I bare my teeth in triumph. The alarm will surely come, but it is already too late.

Tonight, as on the other nights, most of the Senate is meeting, honing their rhetoric on each other. The wise among them counsel accommodation with Hannibal, but most display the intransigence of the Romans, as famous as it is arrogant.

Tonight we go to meet them.

~~~

Our gate is quiet. The fiery arrows and screaming Gauls are concentrated elsewhere this time. But this is Hannibal we face, and nowhere will be left unguarded or unwatched.

We tense as a cart appears, rolling along the road toward us. But it is making no attempt to hide, being lit with a torch and coming toward us down the narrow street between the buildings, the mule driver whistling tunelessly.

"Hail!" he calls when he nears us. "By the generosity of Vincentius, Senator of Rome, tonight we are ordered to travel between the gates, bringing wine to warm the blood of the brave guardians of Rome!"

I signal to two of the men, who silently pad forward to inspect the cart. But there are no hidden men, no hidden weapons. Just the two men in civilian garb, their mule, their cart and its enticing load of barrels. So I allow them to bring it closer. We do not reduce our watchfulness, but nor will we spurn the generosity of our benefactor: even if we suspect it is less generosity than the first step in a campaign to become consul. So after insisting that both men take a healthy swallow of the wine themselves, we cheerfully join in, keeping some to pass to our fellows at the top of the wall later. If all the other guards insist on the same caution against poison, I wonder how many gates these men will actually stagger to tonight.

"Just because the barbarians are howling outside, doesn't mean we Romans can't be civilized, eh?" says one of the men with a wink, and we laugh.

Then the strangest thing happens, so strange that for precious moments we fail to react. The second man casually picks up their torch and waves it beneath the cart as if looking for something, but then thrusts it into the rump of their mule, which brays in shock and lurches forward toward the gate. At the same moment, the man tosses his torch into the air as both men turn and flee as fast as their feet can carry them.

I leap out of the way of the heavy cart.

"A… a… after them!" I cry, picking myself up from the ground, though I am mystified by their actions. If this is an attack, what are they attacking? Their little cart cannot damage our gate even propelled by a startled mule. But as it passes, I see something smoking and flaming beneath it. Do the fools actually think they can set fire to the gate with fire and wine? Madness!

But if a man runs from a dog, the dog will chase him. And if a man runs from the Roman guard he can expect the same. If my men bring them back alive I will ask them their story, and not very gently.

~~~

Our gate is quiet. The fiery arrows and screaming Gauls are concentrated elsewhere this time. But this is Hannibal we face, and nowhere will be left unguarded or unwatched.

Some men approach us, singing and bearing flagons of wine. By their dress and accent they are Roman citizens and freedmen; by their actions, they are either living as if Hannibal were not outside, or perhaps celebrating in defiance of it.

But then the slip of a tunic and a reflection of light reveals a sword, and I cry out in alarm to my men. Maybe the approaching men could still have bluffed their way. But they are not soldiers and they panic. They draw their swords, too soon.

The battle is still fierce, for they are many and desperate. By the time it is over, all but one of our attackers lies dead or wounded; the last, knowing they are lost and seeing his chance, flees. I stand and survey the scene, blood dripping from my sword. Half of my own men lie on the ground, not all moving, and I bitterly curse Hannibal, wondering how much he paid these men to betray their own people.

But you failed, Hannibal. This time you failed. You will find Rome is not so easy to destroy by your tricks and betrayals.

Then it is as if the fist of a god strikes the world, for there is a sound like a thousand thunders, and a giant ball of fire boils up into the sky from the direction of the next gate piercing the wall of Rome.

I fall to my knees in terror, and as I stare up at the burning apparition I wonder if I witness the end of the world.

Or the end of Rome.

CHAPTER 26: ANGELA

A great boom comes from behind the nearest gate and an orange fireball shoots above it, an avatar of war, and my soul quails at what I have done.

The gates are strong, but their strength is mainly directed outward to prevent armies from battering their way in. Breaking out is easier. And as a screaming body of men festooned with sharp implements descends upon a gate now broken and undefended, it takes little time for them to tear it down then flow into the city, a tide of howling death.

As I stare at the fading glow, an old poem about Guy Fawkes floats into my mind:

> Remember, remember!
> The fifth of November,
> The Gunpowder treason and plot;
> I know of no reason
> Why the Gunpowder treason
> Should ever be forgot!

Forgive me.

But I do not know whose forgiveness I seek, or whether I can ever be forgiven.

I had the idea soon after I arrived in Spain with Hannibal. I did not want to do it. I did not intend to use it. But I could, and even though I did not believe I was in the past or could change it if I was, I knew I needed the chance. And so I took it. And so I am damned.

I was fortunate, if being given the means of your own damnation can be called that, for one of my history classes had an assignment on the history and implications of gunpowder, and I had learned how simply it was made. It is about fifteen percent charcoal, easily obtained in this age of cooking fires. It is about one tenth sulfur, easily identifiable and known from antiquity. But the other three quarters is saltpeter, the nitrate salt of potassium, and I wasn't even sure it was used for anything in this era, let alone readily available in useful quantities.

But one thing in plentiful supply is animal manure.

At first I did not tell Hannibal what I was doing. I merely asked him to find me a quantity of sulfur and to assign some assistants for my bizarre manure processing facility. He was intrigued and amused enough at this new addition to my long list of oddities to comply.

It takes a long time to make saltpeter. You need manure, including plenty of urine, throw in wood ash and some straw, keep the rain off and keep turning it for up to a year. Harvest the crystals as they form in their white flowers, purify the nitrate by boiling and filtering, and dry it out.

Fortunately Hannibal had an army of animals, would take a few years before marching off to Italy, and there was plenty of spare land. And so the world's first saltpeter farm began.

I knew Hannibal's patience would not last forever. Manure has other uses, as do men. So one peaceful sunlit day I told him a wanted to go out with him on a picnic, just us and our most trustworthy guards. After we had eaten, I picked up a little bag I had brought with me and addressed Hannibal.

"Husband, I have a gift for you. But before I show you, I need your oath that you will not ask me its secret, nor ever seek to work out that secret yourself. That you will never try to make it or use it, beyond what I do for you."

"Before knowing what it is?"

"You know the tale of Pandora, and how after she opened her urn it was too late to turn back? This is much the same. Afterwards will be too late. You must swear now."

"Is it that important?"

For some reason I shivered and wrapped my arms around myself. "Do you want me to be like Prometheus, tied to a rock for eternity, being eaten alive by vultures for bringing man the fire of the gods? It is that important."

He smiled his most tolerant smile, so I knew I was in trouble. But he said, "I suppose I could torture you to show me without my oath, but you offered me this gift freely and if you had not, no oath would be needed but no knowledge would be gained. So I swear, Angela. I swear by Baal, by Tanit and by my own life, that I will not seek the secret of your gift or use it without your permission."

"Then come with me. The men can stay here. They should not see. Can you bring a burning taper?"

Turning to the men, I added, "Barekbaal! Can you give me your helmet? I'm sure Hannibal will grant you another if anything should happen to this one."

With a puzzled frown at my obscure comment, he handed over his helmet. So armed, we went a little distance then with a flourish I whipped out a small, sealed clay pot with a string poking out of the top. I was being very dramatic today. He looked at it, even more puzzled.

"A pot? And not even a very well made one."

"You will see why. When I light this, we must run to that tree. Agreed?"

I placed the pot on a rock, lit the fuse, quickly placed the helmet over the pot, and then we ran away. The pot was still visible through the face of the helmet and the fuse burned quickly, as I had steeped it in saltpeter.

"Now watch."

The sputtering fuse disappeared into the pot, then there was an almighty bang, the helmet sailed majestically into the air and pieces of pot flew everywhere. The guards came running, swords drawn, but Hannibal assured them all was well.

Then he looked at me, looked at the scorched rock where the pot had stood, looked at the helmet lying on the ground rather worse for wear, looked back at me. Then he spoke hoarsely, "What... what was that?"

"The fire of the gods," I whispered.

I could see the wheels turning behind his eyes, and knew their track and destination.

"With this... but with this... we could be invincible! Why would you show me this, yet make me swear not to use it?!"

I shook my head sadly. "No my lord, it would not make us

invincible. We do not have time to make enough for that. And even if we could, remember Pandora: once it is out we can never put it back. Once men saw this they would all want to know its secret, and you know what men are like: before long they *would* know it. Then instead of wars fought with arrows and swords you would have wars fought with this. Instead of being invincible, we would be back where we were, only using and facing weapons far more terrible than any you have seen before."

"Then why show me? Why tempt me, if you fear it would lead to our destruction?"

"I have something in mind, and I shall tell you when the time is right. But before then I need your help. Will you give it?"

He nodded, but in his eyes behind the shock and alarm I could still see the wheels of his great military mind turning, and I felt afraid. He is an honorable man, my husband Hannibal. But how many honorable men have there been throughout history who have faced a temptation even greater than their honor, and fallen?

And who was I to criticize them, I who had brought gunpowder into a past not ready for it, if indeed the world had ever truly been ready? I who had sought to bring peace, but to do it had brought the shortcut of terror?

We stared at each other, both lost in our own crises of honor and betrayal, promises we made to others and the lies we tell ourselves. Both not thinking it in these terms, but hoping nonetheless, that our honor would be enough to save us from a hell of our own making.

And so I made my saltpeter and carted a large quantity of it, along with the sulfur Hannibal had provided, from Spain across the Alps into Italy. It was borne by Surus, the one elephant I could be sure from history would survive the trek. And then as we overwintered north of the Arno and warmed ourselves before our fires, I collected and ground my charcoal.

Then after we crossed the Arno and Hannibal began his rampage in order to draw the Romans into a battle of his choosing, I stayed in a safe refuge with guards and workers, and set to mixing the ingredients together. Black powder is not ideal. Its parts will separate in transport, and it has other weaknesses. So once my powder was mixed I wet it, compressed it into cakes and dried it in the air and sunshine of Tuscany. Like some farmer drying tomatoes, except mine was a far deadlier harvest. Finally we ground the dried cakes into coarse grains, sealed our lethal cargo to keep flame and moisture out, and rejoined Hannibal's army.

Now the genie I have released upon the Romans has done what I asked, and I pray that I can recall it. What was that Hindu scripture Oppenheimer quoted about his atomic bomb?

Now I am become Death, the destroyer of worlds.

Now I too have unleashed my Hiroshima, and even if it was one gate not one city, its consequences may prove even more deadly. I tremble to think that in my time even a whole city was not enough, and the demon had to descend upon Nagasaki as well to prove it could be invoked more than once. But I have no Nagasaki to follow mine up with, and I pray once will be enough.

CHAPTER 27: CATO

Rage threatens to consume my mind, so I am walking the streets of Rome to burn off my anger. The incursions of Hannibal have brought danger, but danger brings opportunity to the bold, and my noble friend Flaccus had persuaded me to come to Rome. Here I embark on my own Course of Honor, perhaps some day to become one of the great men of Rome.

If there still is a Rome to become a great man of.

I have been observing the Senate. Often enough I am tempted to speak. But at only seventeen years of age, who would listen? Yet still I might speak, and I judge that my influence will be greater if my own passions are under control and my voice is one of calm reason. When you are young, it is too easy for others to dismiss your arguments if you let your heart run your mouth with insufficient diversion through your brain. Even if all those around you are doing the same, or if like too many men, any diversion through the brain has no effect.

It is all the fault of that witch Hannibal brought with him. Hannibal's surprising victories have sowed fear in the city, and his decision to attack Rome on the heels of his slaughter of that fool Flaminius at Trasimene has made it worse. But those of us who retain any sense know that Hannibal has erred. The Gauls might have sacked Rome once before, but we are Romans. We picked ourselves up, then we built a wall. Cowards tremble in fear when each night Hannibal's army attacks a different point of that wall, too foolish to realize that his sole purpose is to induce fear, to turn the fear into panic, and achieve a victory through cowardice that he cannot gain through might.

For there is no way Hannibal can take the city. Our walls are too strong and stoutly defended. Yes, other cities have thought that and still fallen, like mighty Troy of legend. And perhaps if he had long enough Rome might also one day fall. But he does not have long enough. He cannot get in, and it will not be long before we can bring our own armies against him and he must flee or die. His victories have been great, but they have depended on his army's mobility and his ability to choose the place of his battles. Trapped against our walls, he would lose all that and his life with it, and he knows it.

Our people should know it too.

We had heard the stories of the woman. That she could make men fly through the air at her command, raise the dead or kill a man with a glance. Superstitious nonsense! But then the bitch came to us on her elephant, pretending her friendship to Rome, offering us the grace of our surrender. Then she received a shower of arrows as her answer, as she should: and yet she was unharmed.

Those of us with any wisdom left were still not tricked. If she has such great powers, why not break down the walls then and there? Why come only to the extreme end of arrow range, not face the full fury of our defiance? Why cover her face as if afraid of those arrows? Fools blubber that she was casting a spell, and that is why the arrows missed her, as if any cause other than distance is needed to explain it. No, I do not know how she survived the one arrow that struck her. Her indecent attire left room for as little armor as imagination. And yet I saw the arrow strike; and then I saw her pluck it from her flesh, unharmed, and toss it away in contempt.

And in so doing this one woman has unmanned half of Rome.

These thoughts are interrupted when I am nearly knocked over by a rough fellow running around the corner.

"Hey!" I shout at him in anger, but he pays me no heed. Curious, I rush into the street he came from.

I have time only to see a group of guards jumping away from an out of control cart plunging toward the gate, when there is a crash of light and thunder and a pillar of fire and smoke surges above the end of the street! I am thrown backwards and lie there in shock. Shock at what happened; shock at the sight of smoke and fire; shock at the sight, or rather lack of it, of men or cart, now only fragments and bits of bloody burnt flesh. Shock at the sight of the torn gate through the smoke.

Now I feel a worse shock, as I hear a howling mob and see grappling tools clawing at the remnants of the gate. A more familiar style of death. *They knew this was coming!* Then I pull myself to my feet, and run for my life and the life of Rome.

I am young and strong, yet my heart is nearly bursting as I near the Curia. The guards move to intercept me but I gasp out, "I bear news for the Senate!" That and my appearance is enough, and they part to let me through.

I rush inside and fall to the floor. "We are undone!" I cry.

The Senators stop yelling at each other and turn to stare at me in astonishment. One steps forward.

"Explain yourself!"

For long moments I stare at him, until finally I am able to stand and speak.

"The enemy are inside the gates!"

I am met by cries of doubt and consternation. "How is that possible?" one shouts.

"There was… there was… it was as if the gods struck the city! A great flash of fire and peal of thunder struck, and when I could look again, the gate was broken! The guards were just… gone! Gone! All of them! As if devoured! And then the enemy were at the gate, tearing it down!"

"Impossible!"

"You are mad!"

"What shall we do?"

"We must escape!"

"It is too late!"

And it is too late. We hear shouting outside and the clash of arms. I look around at faces full of fear or hate or resolve, but all I see is the image burned into my brain of that fireball of death. And my earlier thoughts return to mock me. *If she has such great powers, why not break down the walls?*

I sink to the floor, no longer able to stand, and I do not know whether it is my injuries or something worse that has robbed me of my strength.

Armed men enter, and they are not Romans, but it is Roman blood dripping from their swords.

My mind goes back to what was our worst day, one hundred and seventy years ago when the Gauls sacked our city and put most of the

Senate to death. Now the Gauls and other barbarians are back in our city, brought here by our enemy Hannibal. I wonder whether we too will die this night and the Rome we have failed will again suffer fire and pillage and rape; and whether two centuries hence children will learn of our fate and again vow 'Never Again'. Or whether there will be no Rome to remember or regret this night.

The warriors who have entered are well behaved. They commit no slaughter, but nor do they say anything to indicate our fate. They are waiting, and we wait with them.

Finally their leader surveys our group and deigns to speak. "I am Maharbal, second in command to the great Hannibal, general of Carthage. So here is the head of the snake that would cast its coils around the whole world! What do you think we should we do with it?"

Some of our number fall to their knees and plead pathetically for their lives, but the soldiers ignore them with looks of contempt. Yet I feel a tinge of pride that most of the Senators are Roman to the last, and whatever emotions haunt their eyes and play across their faces, they stand in quiet dignity.

But I fear the dignity is for show and the emotions tell the truth. For what I see in those faces, and what I am sure our enemies are seeing, is fear. And the fear itself is mere paint over a panic awaiting its chance to emerge. Most look ready to obey the first man to give a command. Some glare at our enemies with hatred, but it is a hatred that dares not express itself anywhere beyond their eyes.

And how do others see me, I wonder? A pathetic youth, collapsed upon the floor? I summon my strength and manhood, and slowly rise, to face my enemies like a man and a Roman: bloodied, defeated, perhaps to die, but never to be conquered.

Then a man enters, and I know I am looking upon the face of Hannibal. Somehow his eyes are drawn to mine as mine are to his, as if in tribute to some future neither of us can see or comprehend.

One of the Senators, one with more hate or perhaps less wisdom than his fellows, bellows a challenge and charges at Hannibal with dagger drawn. Hannibal asserts his authority by calmly cutting him down with his sword.

"Senators of Rome," he cries. "Let us have no more bloodshed! We offered you peace. You chose war. Now you see where it has brought you. Yet we offer you peace again! Your city lies open before us. Now choose whether you and your people live or die!"

One of the Senators speaks. "What are your terms? Perhaps fighting to the death will be preferable."

And by that question, despite the disclaimer to cover it, and by the silence of the others, I know we have lost.

"We seek domain over all islands in the Great Sea. We will agree that Rome may do what it pleases in Italy: but not beyond. Levies of ships to return Carthage to ownership of the seas. Reasonable reparations to pay for our losses. But not so high as to impoverish Rome, as Rome impoverished Carthage: for we do not want Rome to be our enemy, or our vassal, or our victim. We have now both seen where that may lead. We told you the truth. We want Rome to be our friend."

He gazes around the hall, meeting the eyes of each man who retains the courage or the hate to meet his.

"My people the Phoenicians have lived for thousands of years as traders. I see on most of you here the purple that was the foundation of our empire. Rome is strong and Italy is rich, and traders gain by both strength and wealth. We do not wish to fight Rome, or to put Rome in chains so heavy that one day it must rise up in revolt. We wish to be friends who trade goods, not blows."

Then his gaze hardens.

"Order your soldiers to surrender their arms. Agree to my terms. Or you shall all die here, tonight, knowing that your city will burn and your people will die or be sold into slavery: knowing that you are to blame.

"Send for me when you decide.

"Or if you lack the courage to decide, I shall let you live long enough so that your last sight is to see your city and people burn."

He turns and strides away. I remember the tale of how years ago he made a vow to his father never to be a friend to Rome, and I wonder if his offer is breaking that vow. But what is the greater punishment for a proud man? To die in battle, roaring his eternal defiance, or to live on, broken and humbled, with every day a reminder of the glory reached for but lost, and now forever out of reach?

I feel the tears on my face, and know they are not from my wounds.

CHAPTER 28: ANGELA

It has been two years since our return to Carthage, bringing with us a peace treaty, Roman treasure, and numerous hostages from the highest families in Rome. In my mind they were never to be mere hostages. I hope that they will learn the ways of Carthage, and perhaps in their own way help tame the beast that no doubt still slumbers fitfully in the heart of Rome.

In my own history, even with his failure in Italy and his ultimate defeat in Africa that ended the war, Hannibal was admired enough to be elected *suffete*, one of the leaders of Carthage. It is a joint position, much the same as the 'Judges' who once ruled the ancient Israelites, those persistent cousins from the Phoenician homeland of Canaan. As a *suffete* he proved himself as able in government as elsewhere. He rooted out corruption and applied his great mind as effectively to increasing the wealth of Carthage as he had applied it to conquest. Unfortunately for both Hannibal and Carthage, this was as popular with those who had grown fat on the status quo as it usually is, and sadly men like that tend to have more power than morals. So too soon, the jealousies that had plagued his military campaigns caused him to flee Carthage and continue his enmity with Rome in other military theaters until the end of his life.

Now with victory, Hannibal's position was secure, as none would dare move against him; nor was there a victorious Rome to run to with tales of treachery. As his own power grew he decided to remain in Carthage, leaving his brothers to consolidate and extend their holdings in Spain while he grew the strength of the empire from its heart.

Whatever Hannibal's original suspicions and ongoing doubts may have been, he was never an unreasonable man. My role in the final defeat of his ancient enemy Rome was, in his view, sufficient proof of my reliability. And so our own relationship grew in both trust and depth of feeling.

Whatever my own original doubts, the defeat of Rome also freed me from the worst of them. I still suspected I was completely delusional and hoped one day to awake in a nice soft bed to the discovery that it was all in my head. But I no longer feared that fate would expunge me from history or existence itself. If I had somehow arrived in the past, the future from that point was not fixed. Whether I was dreaming, in some alternate timeline or actually living in my own past, my future was now open to me. There is no fate, only choice.

And so I have been making my own plans.

CHAPTER 29: AHUMM

How ironic an end for one of our people, to die on a limitless ocean! Though in truth the irony is less amusing when I have brought so many others to die with me.

Blinded by glory; bewitched by dreams of wealth; deceived by my own hubris. Or was I merely tricked into sailing to our deaths, as if by some kind of reverse Siren, who sang us away from the safety of land into endless seas from which none may return?

I remember how it all started, this ill-conceived expedition. The great Hannibal himself had put out a call for men as skilled on the ocean as courageous in their hearts and flexible in their minds. I come from a long line of merchants, all expert in the arts of the sea. Even the name I proudly bear means 'Brother of the Sea'.

Many heeded his call. Some sail in other ships of our doomed fleet; but it is I who was chosen to lead it, and I who must bear the blame. As it has so many times before, my mind returns to the fateful day that set my destiny.

Intrigued by Hannibal's call I had gone to learn more, only to be told I must first provide a written statement of my abilities. I found it offensive—as who would not?—and almost turned on my heel. Then I remembered the part about a flexible mind and wondered if this was a test. So I gritted my teeth and complied, though when I left I was unsure whether I should care to ever hear about it again. But when I received an invitation to meet with Hannibal himself I felt an unexpected twinge of excitement, and I knew I would go.

I was ushered into a room and found myself under the inspection of not only the great Hannibal but his mysterious and exotic wife, she of more rumor and speculation than fact. I had never seen her so close, and a sudden feeling of recklessness made me meet her inspection with one of my own. As a merchant, I was staggered by the wealth embodied in her purple gown and incredibly fine jewels; as a man, I was intrigued by her striking coloration but startled by the directness of her piercing gaze.

I was more startled when the one who spoke to me was not Hannibal but her.

"Greetings, Master Ahumm," she began. "You are a fine seaman, I understand?"

"Ah... yes, ah... ? I am sorry, my lord," I answered, directing my question to Hannibal, "I do not know how I should address the... your wife."

"You may address her as 'My Lady'," he replied coldly, though the glint in his eyes spoke more of amusement than anger. "No doubt you have heard many things about her. Some of them may be true. In any case it is to her you must answer on this matter."

"Yes, my Lord Hannibal."

Then I turned nervously toward her, clearing my throat. "Ah, yes, My Lady. One of the finest, from a long line of mariners. As you can see," I added, pointing to my written statement that I had spied on the table in front of her.

"Then you are familiar with the Great Sea."

"Of course," I replied, mystified. For who isn't?

"Imagine that I asked you to sail from the straits at its western entrance to Tyre on its eastern coast and back again; perhaps even back to Tyre again. Imagine that I asked you to do this without ever touching land during your journey until it was completed. Could you do it?"

"But what would be the point? It would be folly to never touch land during a voyage of such an extent when land is so close to hand."

She did not answer, just gazed at me as if my comment was beside the point. I glanced over at Hannibal, but his face gave me no clues either. Perhaps this was another test.

"Well, My Lady, it would be difficult. Many supplies would be needed." I paused while I considered the problem. "But yes, I think maybe it could be done. Knowing in advance the problems before us, we could ensure enough food and water were stowed. We might need to hope for some good rain during the voyage, despite that. But we would be very unlucky not to get it. The gods of the sea are capricious, but often favor the bold."

"You would be willing to undertake such a voyage, knowing the risks? Knowing you could not touch land if you wanted to?"

I held her gaze for a moment. "But, My Lady, what would be the purpose?"

"Assume I know more than you and there is a purpose. And at the end of such a voyage lies glory and wealth to you, and eternal glory to Carthage."

A wise man would have said no. A fool in his hubris said instead, "Then I would."

She smiled, and replied, "Then I shall tell you the truth."

She leaned back, ordering her thoughts, then began her strange tale.

"Far to the west lies a great continent. So great it stretches from the southernmost to the northernmost points of the world. So great that if you went far enough west… you couldn't miss it," she added with another smile.

"But in that lies the problem," she continued, her smile gone. "The distance I asked you to travel is the distance you might need to go to reach it. Exactly how far depends on your precise direction. Exactly how long on your direction and what accidents of weather you might encounter, be they storms or their opposite."

I did not know whether to be skeptical or intrigued. I went with intrigued. "But how could you know of this land…?" The words stopped in my throat, as suddenly I saw her strange garb and appearance with fresh eyes. "This… this land is your homeland, My Lady?!"

She gave me a startled look, as if she had not expected such a deduction. I confess to having felt satisfaction to have learned that whatever this woman is she could still be surprised, and it was I who had surprised her. If she wished to test me I would show her my mettle!

"Perhaps one day," she replied in a voice as soft as her reply was obscure.

"But it does not matter how I know," she continued more briskly. "It is enough that I know. The land is there. It is far away, but you tell me not too far away. It is a land of great size and great wealth; rich in gold and other metals, rich in farmland. If Carthage can reach it, it will open up new trade routes and more: new places to build cities. If

Carthage can colonize this new world within our lifetimes, its glory will be eternal."

For a long minute I stared at her, thinking. I looked again at Hannibal, but he was watching us calmly: not as if he thought his wife's tale was the ravings of a madwoman. I decided to grasp the situation and ride it.

"There are no islands between here and there that might ease the journey?"

"There are some but they are few and small. Even if they could assist you, you are likely to miss them entirely. Better not to rely on them and to assume an empty ocean."

"What peoples inhabit this land?"

"None you know. Farmers, hunters and warriors, even small empires with armies, but none of the size and strength once held by Persia or the Greeks. Perhaps most similar to the northern barbarians or the inhabitants of Britain in lifestyle, but dark of hair and brown of skin."

"And their language?"

"Several, but you would recognize none of them."

"Does this land have a name?"

She paused as if in thought, or as if trying to remember a distant time. Then she shrugged. "Amerika. Let us call it Amerika."

"Can you give any guidance to this Amerika better than 'go west'?" Something in my words brought a faint smile to her lips, but she did not explain her reaction.

She showed me a rough map. I recognized our part of the world but she is not a good map drawer, and I felt a twinge of uncertainty. However she knows—or thinks she knows—the things she says, she lacks the all-seeing eyes of a god.

"Here," she pointed, "we are. Here around Iberia toward the north are the isles of Britain. Now attend. I said the journey is long, but there are three shorter routes you might take. You see that to the north Amerika thrusts eastward into the ocean. So the distance is less if you head west from the mouth of the Great Sea and a little to the north. But the land up there is cold. There is also this long chain of islands in the sea near the middle, so if you go west but a little south instead the distance is similar, and they are a much warmer destination. But also see here: farther south, Africa bulges west while south Amerika bulges east, so while the total distance from *here* is similar, the distance you have to sail far from *land* is much shorter, less even than the width of the Great Sea itself. The disadvantage is that first you have to sail a long distance along northwest Africa and there are no cities there; also this part of south Amerika is jungle and perhaps not the richest or best destination. However on both sides of the voyage at least you would be able to hug the land as you travel and hopefully restock with food, water and other supplies. You are the mariner. Which of these routes would you choose?"

Intrigued, I examined the map closely, my doubts held in abeyance as I contemplated the problem. "Yes," I finally answered. "The total distances are much the same, but if we stay close to land until we must strike out across the water our options are much better. And we could get at least some supplies before that most dangerous part as opposed to none. Our main problem is carrying enough supplies. Knowing how many supplies we need is part of the solution, but reducing our needs is even more important. And in the worst case we will have traveled half our distance before we need to leave Africa, so if we hit problems we could simply return the way we came in reasonable safety, not find ourselves stranded at sea unable to make our way back home."

Having caught up with the concept of this great western land, the significance of its own western coastline caught up with me. I pointed to the map. "And what lies beyond this land?"

She laughed, and I looked at her, puzzled. "Oh, Ahumm! Truly you are a Phoenician! I give you half a world, and already you want the rest of it!"

"One other thing," she added, sketching some circles on her map. "As you know winds change, but the general direction of the winds are in two great circles moving in opposite directions," she explained, rotating her fingers over her map. "So they tend to blow west toward your destination here in the middle and east toward home further away. I advise you not to try going south along southern Amerika. That takes you farther from home, and when you return you would have a long voyage back around Africa. Maybe you will learn that the winds will allow you to return the way you came. Or perhaps you can continue north, along the island chain and to north Amerika. There you will find winds to bear you back home. Though the journey is longer it may prove faster. And more profitable."

Then she retraced her finger along the route she had just described. "As I said, if you succeed in reaching this most easterly part of the southern land you will find mostly jungle. There will be people there but I do not know what welcome they will give you. And be warned. There are many strange things in that jungle, and its people may be armed with poisonous darts and arrows, with which they can strike at you from their hiding places if they take a dislike to you. You are expert traders, and if anyone can come to a peaceful arrangement it will be you. But I advise you to stick to the coast. Do not be tempted to strike inland. There is nothing but jungle for more miles than you can count, and the natives might strike you down at any time without you even knowing they are there until you are dead. To you it is a strange jungle filled with swamps and traps. To them it is home.

"And it is not only the natives. This jungle is home to fierce cats, giant snakes who can swallow a man whole, and even the rivers may contain fish that will strip the flesh from your bones.

"But as you go north you will come across greater civilizations. They too are fierce, but more settled, and you might find great opportunities for trade. And if the people even farther north are again less settled, their lands are very rich. If you can befriend them so they welcome your return and even permit you to settle, it may prove to be your greatest achievement of this journey."

At this stage I confess I just stared at her.

"Does your courage now fail you, Ahumm? I would understand if it is so."

"My... Lady," I said hoarsely. "But... my Lady! How do you know these things?! How could you know not only that these lands exist, but their shapes and what lies within? How could you know the direction of the winds across half the world?"

"Master Ahumm," she replied. "If I told you that tale you would not believe it. It is enough that I know it. I will not deceive you: there are many dangers, which I am sure you can imagine for yourself. But I do not deceive you: it is as I have said. Now you may choose to believe me and seek your glory. Or you may choose the safety of not believing me, and return to plying the waters of what you think of as the 'Great' Sea, when one far greater calls to you. The choice is yours."

~~~

And so I made my choice, and that is how I find myself here. The winds have picked up and we still ply west, for what else is there to do? But few now believe that we sail to more than our deaths.

I thought I was wise. Prudent. But my careful planning has come to nothing. First we scouted along the coast of Africa until we could be sure that among the usual meanderings of any coastline we had found its most westerly point. Then we built a settlement in the best nearby location with plenty of water, where we could store goods, grow crops, raise animals and even trade with the local tribes. It will never be the greatest of our cities but it may well prosper in the years to come, when we and our ill-fated expedition have passed into cautionary tales. So perhaps I have left that much legacy behind me.

Then finally the great day came. Our ships had all arrived in port and all had been loaded with as much food, water and trade goods as we could carry. Surely enough of the former to survive the journey, and enough of the latter to make it worthwhile. And so with the sun behind us our ships caught the fair winds and sailed toward the west, seeking the new lands which until then were but promises and hope drawn in lines on papyrus.

So we sailed toward the setting sun but trending southward. Sailing is hard work but the men were of good cheer, facing our exciting future with great anticipation. The weeks wore on. Sometimes the wind would drop, and we would drift with the currents when we could row no more. Other times storms struck, scattering us and putting us off course. One of our ships is lost; we hope they too are still heading toward the promised land and that one day we will meet again.

But it is taking too long. I do not know whether we have been blown or drifted too far off course, or perhaps back over our course. The smell of salt water and the feel of it mingled with sweat is lifeblood to the sailor, but no more. We need land. But all we see is ocean. Perhaps that is all there is. Philosophers say the world is a great ball, but I think they are wrong. Hear me, for who has voyaged as far? The world is a small island of the land we call home adrift in an infinite ocean. It is said that the spirits of the dead journey to the land of Mot, the dread god of death whom none worship but to whom all must one day come. Perhaps we are pawns in a game of gods, stolen away from Mot by Yam, god of the sea; our spirits doomed to forever wander his ocean, ever seeking a land we shall never find.

~~~

I wake. I am thirsty, but that has been my fate and the fate of my men for more days than we can remember. The winds have deserted us but the sun has not. Nor has the ocean, which carries us along where it will. Still we go westward, but trending to the north, having neither the will nor the strength to fight the sea any longer.

I walk the deck, encouraging the men, not letting them see my own despair. Then our lookout shouts and points to the southwest. I climb up to join him and there on the distant horizon is a long, low grey band. Perhaps at last a storm is coming for us and our ordeal will end not in the slow delirium of thirst but in a terror of lightning and waves. But perhaps…

I shout to my men and signal the other ships drifting along in our loose formation of the doomed. Perhaps I am driving us to our deaths. But perhaps that is all I have been doing ever since the tale of the great west land possessed me. But should we just drift until death takes us? No. We are men, and we will fight as men, and if the gods wish to destroy us we will fight them too. My men are barely fit to row. But row we must. And so the creaking of our oars begins to loosen the hold of the sea and our ship turns toward the southwest, no longer a slave to the sea but back under the command of my will.

The smudge on the horizon rises, and I see that it is indeed clouds. But then something darker appears beneath the clouds and the muttering of the men takes on a new tone. Then when the darkness takes on a green tinge, we know it is true: the jungle I had stopped believing in is real.

CHAPTER 30: ANGELA

In another age, I might have been enjoying a Mediterranean holiday, perhaps at a coastal resort, or maybe in a private whitewashed villa on a little island rising jewel-like from the sparkling sea.

In many ways that is now my life. It has become my habit to sit in our rooftop garden, writing, thinking, occasionally glancing out toward the sea. There is something peculiarly relaxing about the Mediterranean, with its warm sun and cooling breezes; a relaxation perhaps ironic given the amount of blood spilled on its shores over its long and contentious history.

So here I sit in the sun, a woman of Phoenicia. I am nibbling on some cheese and bread with the occasional grape or olive. It is not what I would have eaten at home, but I have come to like the diet of my new people; somehow, it goes with the ambience. I have even become used to what they call wine. I take a sip as I rub my swelling belly. Do not judge me. I do not think my small amount of watered down wine will harm the life growing inside me; rather I think my relaxed happiness might benefit his or her growing spirit. In any case far greater dangers to this child arise from the era in which he or she will be born, than from anything I might eat or drink.

A sail appears in the distance and I smile. Months before today, every ship I saw made my heart leap and I would lean forward in hope. But every ship I saw turned into just another ship, and my heart sank. I knew this was irrational. But I was like a schoolgirl waiting for her crush to bring her a rose, and my unruly heart followed hope above reason. Then even my heart learned. For a while I still came up to the roof telling myself it was for the air, even while my eyes would frequently tell me otherwise by scanning the horizon; until at last the ships were just ships.

Ahumm's expedition has been gone a long time now, and I fear too long. I always knew it was risky. They could have been lost at sea, drifting beyond sight of land until all perished. Perhaps they reached the rich land to the west and celebrated their good fortune, only to be lost in a storm on their return voyage. Or maybe they ran afoul of the natives, and now lie dead on foreign soil, or perhaps eke out the rest of their miserable days as slaves to the cruel masters of a strange land.

Now this ship has come closer, and I see the purple flag with a white star waving proud from its mast. And I stand, as if greeting a new future driving through the waves toward me.

Chapter 31: Angela

I am an old woman now. In my era of air conditioning, food whose quality matches its abundance, and medical machines that can peer into the secrets of our bodies, I might be calling this my middle age. Perhaps looking forward to a retirement spiced with cruising around the world to exotic places. But I have cruised to a far more exotic locale than ever I could have imagined, and it is a harsher time. I have lived here forty years now, and I feel its accumulated insults down to my bones.

As we travel through our life, each day has the intensity of immediacy, with the unknown future looming uncertainly before us. Then the future comes, but no sooner has it come than it in turn scatters in our wake like the leaves of autumn. And so it goes on, day after day as it must, until we wonder where it went. How did all that intensity consume us, pass us and become nothing but memory? How can what was yet to come, now lie so far behind us? So it is with my life. So it is for us all.

Yet there are many moments burned in my memory, and I can relive their joy and terror as if they were mere moments ago. The day I stepped into the past and met Hannibal. The night of my marriage to that near mythic figure of history. The time I rode an elephant to face the arrogant might of Rome. The night I unleashed a hell from the future that helped bring the fall of Rome. That sparkling day when the first ship from America returned from over the horizon.

Those are the moments, sparkling like jewels in the stream of my life. When I look back on my life here I remember the fear of my arrival, the fear of daring to fight Rome, the terror of facing them at the walls of their own city. Then I remember the glory. I remember our triumphant return to Carthage, the city for which we fought and which once had given such lukewarm support to Hannibal: now welcoming us as heroes. And so our wealth and power grew, at the center of what had become the greatest empire in the world. The empire I had helped create.

We bartered our success into the expensive and risky exercise of an expedition to America, knowing it might fail, hoping that we could keep trying until it succeeded. Knowing we had to try, because that was the surest and perhaps only way to win the future I sought.

Then that ship returned. With the discovery of America, the empire of the Phoenicians rose to its zenith. New cities began to grow so far from my new home, and from those points exploration, trade and new cities began to spread through the new world. It all seems so long ago now.

For I am an old woman now.

I am dying. I do not know of what, and there is no medicine here that can either identify or cure my ailment. But I can feel death coming in my bones too. I have been delirious on and off for a few weeks; today the fever has unexpectedly broken, and I feel a strange clarity in its place. Or perhaps my imagined clarity is a mirage, just another face of my delirium. My children have been called. But they are children of Phoenicia and are far away. I do not think I shall see them again, and I grieve at the thought: as if it is I who have lost them; as if it is they who are dying not I.

I look up at the small rocky hill above our villa. Dark storm clouds are gathering, announcing their intent with faint rumbles from far away, and I feel the hairs on my arms lifting. It reminds me of something, and then I remember a night far away. I look at the gilded sword on the wall, then at the chest on the floor, unopened for so long now.

I know what I must do, or think I know: perhaps it is death's way of calling me. I open the chest. Within it lies my purple robe and its accompaniments, still glorious. As the rain begins, I strip off the clothes of a dying old woman and don the clothes of a goddess. Alas, nothing can change the dying old woman they enfold.

I imagine that what I am about to do will kill me, quickly or slowly I do not know. But it seems better to leave this world as I arrived, or at least to try. Perhaps there is no longer any purpose to the legends around me. Perhaps they have achieved all there is to achieve. But I am not doing it for others. I am doing it for myself. My time is ending; let me choose my manner of leaving. Too few of us win that privilege.

Not for the first time I wonder if I have done right, or should be named the worst criminal in history, if there were any with the knowledge to so name me. I think of the greatness of Rome in my world: not of the violence of its growth and preservation, but the glory and peace it brought throughout so much of the world. I think of the great emperors who will never be: of Augustus, Trajan, Hadrian and Aurelius. Yet I also think of the monsters who will never be: of Tiberius, Nero, Caligula and so many more. On the scales of history, will these balance out? Will the empire of Carthage be any better? Or will it too, long after my death, carve out its own legacy of horror?

I have done what I thought was right. Is that enough to save me? Who am I, to act as judge and executioner over history? I wonder whether I should have thrown myself into the harbor of Carthage the day I arrived, rather than preserving my life and pursuing my goals at a price I could never know. We humans, like all other living creatures, cling so stubbornly to our lives, and fight so urgently for the goals that define them. Are we right to do so? But how can there be any other right, than life's reverence for itself? Or its fierce determination to fight the eternal dark that is its only alternative; to carve out and hold its little circle of light and joy in the midst of that night?

The fever has made my memories foggy, but I remember a part of my last conversation with Hannibal, he who was first my protector, then my husband and at last my love. I suppose that as I felt my end coming, I needed an affirmation of my life.

"We have done well, haven't we, my lord Hannibal?"

He smiled. "Carthage is strong and growing, an empire of trade around the world; Rome is contained and at peace. Is that not well?"

I smiled back. The way he put it made me feel like some hero of Greek legend. "Yes, we have done great things, my love. I pray it will be enough, for I have little time now to do better if it is not." And then moved by some unknown need, I recited to him a poem, what I could still remember of one I had known in my youth:

Death closes all: but something ere the end,
Some work of noble note, may yet be done,

Not unbecoming men that strove with Gods.
'T is not too late to seek a newer world.
To sail beyond the sunset, and the baths
Of all the western stars, until I die.
It may be that the gulfs will wash us down:
It may be we shall touch the Happy Isles,
And see the great Achilles, whom we knew.
Tho' much is taken, much abides; and tho'
We are not now that strength which in old days
Moved earth and heaven, that which we are, we are;
One equal temper of heroic hearts,
Made weak by time and fate, but strong in will
To strive, to seek, to find, and not to yield.

He listened intently, though he could not have understood a word, for I spoke it in its original English. Perhaps it is like music, or a song in another tongue, where the sound and the cadence strike our souls at a level more primal than that of concepts and meaning.

He was silent a long time after I finished, then asked softly, "What was that?"

"It is a poem from my world," I replied simply. Then I repeated it in his language, as best I could, so he could also know its meaning in addition to its music.

But now I think of it again, and I know it is a poem that will never be written. History is contingent, chaotic, unpredictable. Why did I, a historian, not act accordingly, and leave well enough alone? Someone once wondered what inestimable number of monkeys typing would be needed to recreate the works of Shakespeare. My actions here have cost many lives, saved many more; changed the paths of migration of men and nations. What chance is there that Tennyson will ever exist now, or recreate that poem in this rerun of history? And how could he, if he did live? English itself is a mongrel hybrid of Latin filtered through other cultures along with German languages and more. There will be no Roman empire to push Latin throughout the world; and who knows what waves of people speaking what tongues will now wash over the isles of Britain in the eternal migrations of humanity?

Nor is that all of my guilt. Now, there will be no Renaissance. There will be no Leonardo. No Michelangelo. No Galileo. The great geniuses of my age, never even dust. And how could there be an England, without the conditions that produced it? There will be no Elizabeth. The great works of Shakespeare will never be written. No Newton, perhaps the greatest scientific mind of all time.

Surely other poets and artists and scientists will arise to take their place. Perhaps they will be even greater. Or perhaps I have destroyed far more than I can ever calculate or know.

I smile at the thought that at least the bitcoin party people will approve of me, for where they dreamed of a New Phoenicia I have saved the old. But with that memory the full enormity of what I have done suddenly becomes real to me. I realize that my guilt is too small. With a historian's eyes I have been seeing only the great people and events of my past, the giants who moved history. They stand like lighthouses above the mass of humanity, their light visible across millennia. But those geniuses and heroes were not alone; alongside them lived the forgotten millions. Forgotten by us, but they too had their own lives and loves, as precious and irreplaceable to themselves as our own always are.

Then at last I see the true meaning of the words I thought so long ago, on the night I rained fire and death upon Rome. *Now I am become Death, the destroyer of worlds.* What I did to Rome was such a small thing compared to the whole.

I remember that party, all the people there, so brilliantly alive as they dreamed of changing the world. But then I changed the world, and now they are all dead: more than dead, for they will never be born. And not only them, but everyone. I have killed my whole world, and so many generations before it: billions of people who can now never be. Now all that remains of them is a memory in the lone mind of their destroyer, thousands of years before their time. A destroyer who soon enough will join them in the dark.

How can I look at what I have done, and live?

In my own time I rejected the God of the Christians. I still believe in no gods, not in my mind; but my heart has absorbed something of Phoenicia. I stand, taking the gilded sword into my hand, resting its blade on my other palm; as it turn it, golden fire runs along its surface. I look out at the driving rain and flashing lightning of a storm still not at its peak. Its growing wildness makes me I feel as if I am facing the vengeful gods of this age, finally come to claim me. Now I am bringing myself before their court, begging no forgiveness, seeking only their wrath. For justice cannot be denied, not in this world or any other.

I take up the sword and walk out. Hannibal sees me approach and looks at me in surprise; but something in him knows, and after leaping to his feet he stands in silence, gazing at me. He asks no questions, but I answer anyway.

"The storm calls me, my lord Hannibal. I go to my fate."

"I do not wish you to go."

"Neither of us can change that, my lord. In your time you have commanded armies and nations, but no man can command this."

He inclines his head, and I walk past him. But at the doorway I stop, then run to him, if my method of slightly faster locomotion can be called running. He enfolds me in his arms as I enfold him in mine; he does nothing, except hold me and stroke my hair, until my quivering sobs cease. Then I give him one long, last kiss, and he lets me go. I turn one more time at the doorway, to see him once more, and see him still standing there, gazing at me as if trying to hold me in reality by burning me into his memory. Then I turn back to the storm.

I am soaked within seconds, but I do not care. Now I stand on the hill, on its highest point, and look up to the raging heavens above. I look at the gilded sword in my hand, thinking that gold is one of the better conductors. I wonder if the carbon nanotubes of my dress are of the conducting type; I think of the water drenching me from head to toe; and I laugh at the thought of what an excellent lightning rod I have become.

Then I lift my sword with both hands, pointing it to the sky, remembering the painting in my apartment from a lifetime ago. What am I doing, part of me wonders? Why do I reach for the lightning, as the woman in my painting reached for the moon? Is it to call down my own judgement for what I have done, in tribute to a painting that will never be painted, by an artist who will now never be born?

In final homage to that painting I strip off my clothes, standing naked in the rain, the robe around my feet. The part of my brain wondering what I am doing has given up, it is now me and the storm and my sword aimed at the sky, and whether I die of lightning or pneumonia no longer matters.

"Then take me!" I cry out to the storm above and the stars above it, anger suddenly blazing through my veins. Rage at whatever power brought me here to this time, and gave me a power I never sought or deserved or knew how to use. But beneath that, I know it is fury at myself for how I did use it.

"If you want me, take me! You put me here! What did you want of me? Nothing? Something? Condemn me if you will! Forgive me if you will! I am a woman out of my time, and now I am out of time, and at last this world will be rid of me!"

My world becomes a coruscating white blaze. I do not know how I can see anything, for surely I am dead, but what I see are a pair of eyes, sparks of white lightning reflected in irises surrounding pits as black as night and deep as infinity, as final as death; and I wonder if I stare into the face of God. Then I fall into those pits and am gone.

CHAPTER 32: HANNIBAL

Eight years. That is how long I have breathed since my Angela left me.

I built a shrine there, at the place she stood the last moment I saw her alive. It is only a small shrine, of white marble; an eight-sided structure with an arch penetrating each side, and benches around its inside walls where a man can sit in thought, or lie down looking up at the heavens that took her; for while there is a roof over the edges, its center is open to the sky.

I now walk with a staff, my legs failing me; shortness of breath has begun to plague my steps. I ignore them and make my way to the shrine tonight without aid, as I do every year in remembrance of her.

We are not now the strength which in old days... Yes, I remember the poem she told me that day, mere days before she left me; even more true now than it was then, when it was already true enough.

A poem from my world, she called it, and after she had recited it to me and translated it for me, I was silent. Finally I asked the question I had always wondered, even though I knew she would not respond, as she had always never responded.

"And where is your world?"

Yet this time she answered.

"I suppose you deserve to know. What harm can it do now? And if you think me mad for it; well, perhaps I am. But perhaps you will forgive me, believing the fever speaks."

She took a deep breath, then continued.

"I came here across time, a time more than two millennia hence. I do not know how. I do not know why, or indeed if there was a 'why'. Perhaps I was brought here by the lightning. Or perhaps it is all a dream, and none of this exists except inside my own brain. In my world you entered Italy. You not only won the battle of Lake Trasimene, after that you won an even greater one at Cannae, crushing two legions of Rome. But even after losing sixty thousand men Rome would not surrender or make terms. Still Rome swore to keep fighting until the last man. It was not what you expected. And it was your end. You, alone with your small force in their country, denied aid from home by the Romans or your own government; for all your skill you could not win. Rome wore you down. Until finally they brought the battle to Carthage itself and you had to return home. And there even you were defeated, by a Roman general as good as you, forged by you, a survivor of Cannae."

She stopped, staring into space at some vision of her own.

"Two generations later, Rome decided you were too troublesome and laid siege to Carthage. Weakened, within only three years it fell, and the Romans destroyed it utterly. What was left of the Carthaginian empire was absorbed by Rome. That was the final end of Carthage, which would never rise again. Many of your people remained scattered around the sea, but of their nation nothing remained."

I looked at her, aghast. She had said things like this when we first met but I never truly believed them; could not believe them. Now after the years we had been through together I was no longer so sure.

"Rome became the greatest empire in history. It owned the Mediterranean. It owned your homeland of Canaan, the top of Africa, Europe from there all the way to Britain. It never owned the world. But it owned enough. You will not believe me, but despite their violence and their greed, still they made a great civilization, whose influence lasted even to my time, though the empire itself had long fallen.

"And I... I came here. And because I believed that an empire of trade must be better than an empire of war, I decided to help you. At first I didn't believe any of this was more than some fevered dream. Then I didn't believe I could change history. But then I did. Because of my arrogance, I destroyed the greatest empire ever, and changed history forever. Not by myself, but still because of me. Even if the world will become a better place, still I destroyed so much glory that it cannot be counted. I am damned for all eternity."

I stared at her, uncertain of what to say. Was she mad, as she thought? But all the things she had done, her unexpected knowledge and her odd ignorance, gnawed at me. I could not believe it. But nor could I say it was not so.

I patted her hand. "I do not know what is true. But if you have changed the world, you have made it a better place. I think the world will thank you, not condemn you."

She smiled at my assurances, not really believing them; but I feel she was comforted just the same, for then she fell back into a gentler sleep.

I looked at her sleeping for a long time wondering, as I had wondered for many years, what she truly was. It was a warm night and we had laid her in the courtyard to enjoy the freshness of the soft breeze; a ray of moonlight lit her face and I wondered whether it was bringing her peace. She had an affinity with the moon, and in my weaker moments I had often imagined that she was a goddess, or perhaps mere messenger, of that light. There was her pale skin and the way she covered herself in the sunlight. It was not modesty, because she felt no need to cover herself in the evening or in low sunshine: but she avoided the bright sun whenever she could; if she failed, her skin would redden, as if the gentlest touch of the sun burned her. So much like the moon itself, chased by the sun on their dance around the world, fading to nothing when the sun caught it, reaching its full glory only when it was farthest from the sun.

I thought at first she might be a priestess of the moon. I had not heard of a cult quite like hers, but if there is one thing we Canaani know it is that the world is wide and there are more gods than there are nations, and within that, almost as many beliefs as there are men. I had been surprised on our wedding night to discover I was not the first man who had bedded her. Not all priestesses are virgins; in numerous cults the temple priestesses engage in holy congress with the worshippers. But still I had been surprised, for her pale fragility and serenity spoke of a purity beyond such carnality, even a sacred one.

I had asked her about this, and she had laughed. Not unkindly or in mockery, but it seemed in simple amusement at the idea of her as either a virginal priestess or its opposite.

"No," she had said, "I am neither priestess nor virgin. But fear not, new husband of mine, nor am I married or a common whore. It is just that in my world, for an unmarried woman to lie with a man is neither unusual nor frowned upon."

In her unguarded moments she had used that phrase occasionally before, 'my world', but I paid it little heed at the time as I found myself doing the frowning her world had neglected.

"Why did you not tell me this?" I demanded.

She looked at me in surprise, then surprisingly blushed. "I... well, it never occurred to me that I should! Do not forget, husband, that I did not seek to marry you, nor did I make any claims. You wished to marry me, knowing that I am not a normal woman: *because* I am not a normal woman. But forgive me, if forgiveness is needed. The last thing I desire is for this to come between us."

"Come between us? And what now? Do you expect your freedom to continue?"

She blushed again. "No, husband. Even in... where I come from, that is usually frowned upon. Do not fear, I shall not shame you. You are the only man who has had me since I arrived in Carthage, and it shall remain so."

I admit my mind was reeling, perhaps in shock at the peculiar customs she accepted so innocently, perhaps in shock that they applied to my own wife and she showed embarrassment but no shame. Then another question intruded into my mind.

"So... how many? How many men have you been with?" I asked harshly.

Her eyes widened and she blushed a third time. "Only a few, but more than one. That is all I shall tell you."

For a moment I was angry, but I reminded myself of the truth of her earlier words; and of my own resolution to suspend normal judgement from this enigmatic being. Instead I asserted my power, or the power I imagined I had, my husband's right over her body; and she responded with unreserved delight. Perhaps her people's customs had their virtues after all.

And now the truth, or the truth as she told it, was even less believable than her divinity.

I am not an especially devout man. I have seen many battles. All men pray to their gods but they live or die regardless. Perhaps I am wrong. Perhaps their fates reflect the secret battles of the gods, and the man who gives no respect to any god is doomed by all. Yet it does not seem that devoutness or even virtue has anything to do with who will live to die an old man surrounded by his children, and who will fall in battle before his life has truly begun. The only virtues that matter in this life are strength of arms, skill to guide the strength, and the spirit to channel both. Even that is not enough, for too many times I have seen the bravest and best fighters felled by an arrow no man could see or avoid; or, skillfully parrying one thrust, slain by another. And as it is true for each man, so it is true of each battle, and so it is true of each war. The best plan of battle can fail, perhaps for as small a reason as one man in the line falling at the wrong time. Perhaps that is how this man, this Scipio, defeated me in Angela's world; or perhaps at last I met a better warrior. I suppose I shall never know.

But for all that my belief in gods lies loose upon me, and I scorn those who believe too deeply, I could never fully dismiss the feeling that in some way by being touched by Angela I had been touched by something divine. And even if it were true that she had come from another world or another time, who but the gods could have done it?

And then came that night when she awoke into some other kind of fevered dream, and appeared before me in her old glory, as if it were I who were dreaming. She bore the sword she had won from the Roman tribune, so many years ago, which I had gilded for her in tribute to what she had done: even though, or perhaps because, her actions that day had at first angered me. She intended to enter the storm outside, and I intended to stop her: but something in her manner forbade me.

I knew one day she would be taken from me. I knew it would be in the night. But I had expected it on a moonlit night. I had even dreamed of it. In my dream she had stood under the light of a full moon bathed in its light, and I had held her; yet I could not hold her and she had dissolved in my arms until nothing remained but the night, the moon and the stars. Yet now she walked out into a storm, her body bowed with age and infirmity, her steps halting. The moon was there, somewhere, I knew: somewhere far above the lightning. Then I remembered how she had wondered whether the lightning had brought her here. Perhaps now, her task and her life ending, it had come to take her back.

And so I watched her walk through the rain to this point on the hill. Strangely, as she walked her body seemed to grow straighter, her steps firmer, as if whatever called her to her fate was granting her this one last gift of strength to bear it. I watched her strip to her skin and stand fearless and alone, sword pointed at the lightning above, crying out to the gods or the storm in her strange tongue. Watched as a mighty bolt struck her where she stood. For a long moment it seemed I could see a dark writhing shadow in that terrible light, but when I could truly see and hear again, she stood there no more.

I hurried to where she had been, but there was nothing left. No body, no gown: just the sword she had held, lying upon the stone she had stood upon, a stone now split asunder by the lightning's rage. It was as if she had told the truth, and as she had come to my world from another, now in death she had at last been erased from mine.

I picked up the sword, now somewhat bent and burnt, much of its gilt melted away, and I made my own plea to the uncaring heavens.

"Then take me too!" I cried. "Take me!" Wondering if the lightning would strike me as well. But I knew the moment had passed. The storm still raged, but its peak was over; and I knew the lightning would not strike here again. I did not know how much of the wetness of my face was rain, and how much tears, nor how long I stood there, alone in the storm, until my servants came to urge me back to shelter.

The sword is still here. I had its point thrust into the cleft rock upon which she had stood, and there it still stands today in mute testimony to her life and how it ended.

And now I look up into the heavens. Tonight no storm rages, and the pinpoints of the stars shine down from the velvet night, a bright crescent moon ascendant, the minor stars hidden by her silver glow.

Did you really cross the ocean of time to be with me, I wonder? What a strange voyage, to what a strange shore, it must have been. Then my eyes grow heavy, and I kneel before her sword and close my hands around its hilt, and rest my head upon the metal of the last thing she held on Earth. Then I sleep.

I dream strange dreams, and am unsure whether they are dreams. Perhaps through the touch of my flesh on her sword I am linked to her spirit across the centuries, and through that link I see visions of the future she created. Or perhaps all I see are her own dreams. For I see the empire of Carthage across the ocean in Amerika growing, a network of cities spreading north and south along the coast and inland, first along the rivers and then inching across the fertile lands and forests. It spreads east as well, east from our ancient homeland until it passes even where the great Alexander was forced to stop by the powers residing there. Those powers do not always welcome us either; but as the centuries pass, more and more see the benefits of a trade that seems to span the world.

My people were never an empire. Never gathered under one ruler. Its cities and states competed as much as they cooperated; even fought on occasion. Angela spoke of an empire of Rome, won and ruled by Rome's legions; an empire forged of iron. The world of Carthage is a net: a net of trade bound by the exchange of wealth. Do you know the fable of the oak and the reed? The oak is mighty and it stands before the storm, indomitable; the reed bends with the wind, appearing weak. But one day the oak will face a storm beyond even its power to withstand, and it will shatter. Rome, Angela said, had fallen despite its glory. I imagine I see similar stresses in the new world of my dream. Wars are still fought. Barbarians from beyond the edges of empire invade. Not understanding civilization, they see glory and wealth and seek to take it; and sometimes they succeed. Like the fate of her Rome itself, writ small.

On one occasion a dire darkness attacks from the east, and coils itself into the heart of our lands like a dragon. From its lair it threatens the cities around it, which begin to quiver and fall. But first a trickle, and then a river, of aid comes from across the seas. The dragon is first annoyed, then enraged, but finally driven from our lands.

And so it continues. Though the glowing network that is the empire of trade might shudder, and parts might darken for a while, it is too resilient. Where one part might fail another remains mighty, and never does night descend upon the whole world. Rome grew, and stood astride the world, facing those around it with its walls of spears and iron: but it could not last. The empire of Carthage is not taken by fire and held by iron to bleed a river of gold to its heart, but enriches all who join it. All the greed and lust and violence of men cannot tear it apart, for to fight an empire of trade is to fight oneself. And whoever might arise with dreams of empire to feed their dark lust for power, its cities are too distant, proud and powerful to rule. And so while storms of darkness still wash across it, slowly our empire stretches to the west and the east until it encircles the world.

Then it is as if the world pauses for breath. As if the task of history is done, and now the world may rest, and there is no need for war or restlessness, just peace. As if no more striving is needed or welcome, for the world is won. Then from I know not where comes a spark that ignites the Earth anew, and the world becomes a blaze of shining light.

I awake, and marvel at what I have seen. I feel a burning in my chest, of exhilaration and vindication. But then the burning blazes fiercer, my breath struggles, and it is as if the sword I touch has been plunged into my chest. I try to cry out, but cannot. Then I know that I am about to depart on my own final journey, along that dark road all men must travel. My strength deserts me and I fall to the ground, rolling on to my back, one hand still grasping the sword: my last link to my past and my love. As I lie there I look up at the night and the moon, still calmly sailing above all the frantic concerns of men. I wonder if it is the moon that calls to me. I wonder what I shall find when I go.

I wonder if my Angela will be there.

CHAPTER 33: SHIMON

A man came to see me today. He hailed me from outside my house, and though I am old, my steps are slow and my eyes grow dim, there was something in his voice which commanded me to come.

I have heard that voice of command before. And though I am frail, and though my body wishes only rest, I obeyed it as I had so many years before.

I looked at the man, and knowing who he was and seeing the cast of his face, my heart knew what his words would be.

"My father Yeshua is dead."

I lowered my head. "Then I will come."

"I knew you would, Shimon the Rock, and have brought an ass to aid you."

I nodded. He helped me prepare for the journey, then helped me sit upon his ass, and then he led me down the road toward Yeshua's home.

We did not speak on our journey, each lost in our own private grief. Men seek to live long, but there is nothing in this world or the next that is without price. And this is the price of a long life, as we watch those we love fall off its road one by one, and with each one the world grows steadily colder.

I remembered the first time I had heard that voice which could not be denied. My brother Andreas and I were young men then, much like my companion today, and we were fishing, when this man with eyes of dark fire bade us to follow him, for he would make us fishers of men.

And so we did, and so began the greatest adventure of our lives.

We thought we would change the world. We thought his Kingdom would come to Earth. We thought so many things, as the young so often do.

It is a strange country, our land of Judah, our people always fractious, as much fighting with each other as proudly despising our enemies even while they rule us. And in my life it has been so strange to be ruled by our ancient enemy, the far descendants of the Kingdom of Tyre, which the prophet Ezekiel foretold would fall and never rise again. Perhaps he was right, for who can gainsay a prophet of the Lord? But if Tyre never rose again, still its seeds were planted elsewhere, and then one day they came back to our shores as the mighty empire of Carthage. Their rule, if rule it is, is light. They have installed a Governor, yet our own people still sit on the throne of Jerusalem, and join with Carthage as much for gain and protection as out of fear of retribution. But they are corrupted by the wealth of Carthage, and have forgotten the ancient ways. And so the Governor does little else than keep his steely eye on the interests of Carthage and adjudicate the most serious of crimes.

This is what Yeshua fought against.

He would cut through the layers of rote phrases and mindless ritual, and penetrate to the heart of the matter and the souls of men. Our people care more to eat the right foods and follow the proper rituals than they care to seek the right values and live the proper virtues. Too many would recoil with horror from the flesh of the pig even while they lust over the flesh of their neighbor's wife.

This is what Yeshua saw. This is what he fought against.

He cared more about men's souls than their bodies. For is not the cleanliness of the body a mere symbol and enabler of the virtue of their souls? Why then do so many value the symbol more than the reality?

This is what Yeshua fought against. He taught men that the Kingdom of God was within, and that to gain the whole world, in all its wealth and approval, meant nothing if you lose your soul along the way. Truth, not appearance; substance, not ritual; love for a man's character, not judgement of his race; reality, not lies. This is what he stood for.

His words angered those who wear fine clothes and strut about the town, hoping their finery will hide the rot within their souls. For they do not want that finery to be pulled back to show their corruption to the world. And Yeshua would spare no man. If you were an honest man you had nothing to fear from him, and that was true whether you were rich or poor, master or slave, man or woman, Jew, Samaritan or Gentile. But if you were not, Yeshua would not spare you the lash of his tongue and the incorruptible judgement of his burning eyes.

An honest man has nothing to fear from the virtuous. And the virtuous have nothing to fear from an honest man.

But there are too few honest men.

It is strange, is it not? How different men can see the same person, saying the same words: and in some he raises hate, in others he raises love, while yet others move by in blank indifference. Those who can see, let them see. The blind do not matter.

Or they should not, and yet too often they do. For Yeshua angered too many powerful men whose gold outweighed their virtue. And so they twisted his words and called him, he whose life was dedicated to God, a blasphemer. They accused him in order to hide their own sin. And the darkest secret of their souls is that they did it to hide it from themselves.

The mob who once adored him, fickle as men so often are, turned against him. And so he was taken by the Temple Guards, beaten and brought before the representatives of Carthage.

They love their fine clothes and perfumed hair, these men of Carthage; their rich silks and soft shoes. It was night when the priests dragged Yeshua to them for judgement, as if even they dared not show their crimes to the light of the sun. I had hidden myself in the crowd who followed them and I remember that night, and will remember it to the end of my life. It was dark, and the flickering flames of torches made dancing shadows in the darkness, as if invoking all the demons of Hell to bear witness to this crime posturing as justice. And in that trembling light it seemed to me as if they had brought my master before a crueler assembly. The Governor's face took on harsher lines, and his guards appeared as men of iron, stern and beyond the call of mercy.

I do not know what happened that night. Perhaps it was my own terror, or perhaps my terror for Yeshua, or perhaps it was just the flames and darkness. But it appeared to me as if in a vision of two worlds colliding: one world of an iron boot laid on the throat of our nation, and another of cynical money-seekers ruling by the seduction of greed rather than the point of a spear. I felt as if a terrible fate had gathered around the man thrown to the floor in the center of the crowd, as if both doom and greatness waited to descend upon him. That he faced a doom that would destroy him yet, in destroying him, transform the world—for good or ill, I could not tell.

"Dead, you say? You want this man dead? Why, what is his great crime, that you want his death and bring him to me in the darkness to get it?"

"He blasphemes against our God!"

"And what is this blasphemer's name?"

"He is Yeshua of Nazareth. For years he has been wandering our land, stirring up the people. He treats our best men with contempt, while making his friends among thieves and whores. An now he claims to be the Son of God!"

"A remarkable man indeed, to be so dangerous yet never before come to my attention. You! Yeshua of Nazareth, what do you say?"

"I speak only the truth."

The Governor clapped his hands and laughed. "The truth! Shall I exile your blasphemer to Greece? The philosophers have been arguing for years about what is truth, and every one of them has a different answer! Ha, ha! If you know the truth, maybe you are as dangerous as they say! Are you dangerous, Yeshua of Nazareth?"

"The truth is always dangerous. Else I would not be here."

"An interesting defense for a man whose life is in my hands. Tell me, prophet, what do you think of Carthage?"

"It is an empire enslaved to Mammon, which seeks gold and fine silk above a pure soul, and God will humble you for your arrogance."

The Governor gave him a searching glance, and in a voice gone dangerously low asked, "And you, prophet? Do you seek to help your God perform this humbling? Would you be King of the Jews, and cast us from your land?"

"My Father in Heaven needs no help. It is men who need help, and I seek only the saving of their souls."

The Governor stared at him, then turned to stare at his accusers for long moments.

For those long moments the flames continued to flicker as a chill wind blew through the hall, and the two worlds I saw seemed to dance with them. Then the Governor sighed, and it was if with his sigh Fate itself took a breath, and moved on.

"I find no ill in this man. Release him!"

"But you heard him!", cried the Chief Priest. "He condemns himself out of his own mouth! He condemns Carthage!"

"Enough! He says nothing more than you say yourselves, only he has the courage to say it to my face!

"I am weary of this land, of you people who are so willing to kill each other over your differences in opinion about a god most of the civilized world hasn't even heard of! I will hear no more of this!"

He glared at the assembly a while longer, as if daring anyone to make further objections.

"But I will have no further disruption in this city! Yeshua of Nazareth, I recommend you go home quietly. Priests, if he will not leave Jerusalem of his own will, you may drive him out with sticks and dung if you please, but I will not have you harm him. If you do, it will be your heads on the pike! Do you understand me?"

Then he swept from the hall in a fog of angry perfume, ignoring the mutterings of the priests, which were carefully set at a volume where he could not hear their words.

Then he turned. "And be warned! You have sought this man's death at the excuse of him despising Carthage! So be careful you do not despise my words yourselves!"

Then he was gone.

The priests looked angrily at Yeshua. They gave him no chance to leave peacefully, even if he would have or could have after their beating, and drove him roughly from the city. Though it was night, still a large crowd accompanied them, jeering and throwing whatever waste they could find. And so they threw him out a minor gate, spat upon him, kicked him, then with a final glare in his direction slammed the gate and locked it against him, a final seal of the city's rejection.

It is to my eternal shame that I said nothing. I told myself it was so that I could help him when most needed. But I knew it was in simple animal fear. That whatever the Governor's words, many men died in this city for many reasons, and while Yeshua's death would bring down retribution, if the priests chose to take out their anger on his followers few would know and fewer would care.

The sight of that gate closing on my friend's crumpled body will never leave me. It closed on a part of my soul.

When we made our way outside we found Yeshua sitting up weeping, but we did not know whether he wept for himself or Jerusalem. We helped him to his feet and he supported his weight on my shoulder. Then he turned to face Jerusalem.

"My disciples, my brothers, my friends. Do you remember just a few days ago when we entered Jerusalem? How the crowds cried out for us and cast palm leaves at our feet? Now you see what men are made of. Where are the crowds now? As happy to spit on us and cast us out as they were to adore us."

"What shall we do?" asked one of us.

"I shall continue. Let those who have ears to hear, hear."

And so we left Jerusalem and continued our ministry. But it was as if the tide which had carried Yeshua to the pinnacle of his glory had broken on the fickle crowds of Jerusalem, and the multitudes began to turn their hearts and minds to other things. Sometimes I would think of my vision that night, and wonder whether, if that tide had broken Yeshua instead, it would have carried his death and his message until it swallowed the whole world. But neither the doom nor the greatness I had tasted that grim night had descended upon him. In that I am weak, as men are, for I was glad he lived. Glory always seems shinier when we see only the glory, not its price.

I sometimes dream, and wonder where the dreams come from. I dream of my vision, of a wilder world, a world ruled by iron, a world that gave my friend a martyr's death. A world where the downtrodden, sharing his pain, would flock to share in his glory; a world where the more our voices were silenced, the louder we would roar; a world where one day even the conquerors would be conquered, not by swords but by words. Not this world of Mammon, the money-worshippers of Carthage; men who do not bother to fight us, but ignore us in casual contempt. The world of men who live for this life only, not the next. The world of men who do not care.

On those nights I wake weeping, and I know not why.

Yeshua never gave up his ministry, but he too moved to other concerns, as if a part of his spirit had broken on the walls of Jerusalem. He went to live with his wife Miriam, where they raised their children, one of whom was by my side today. He still taught, but weary of the deafness and inconstancy of men, he taught only those who cared enough to come to him.

In his life he reached many men and many women, and while his words have not conquered the world nor have they been lost, and so many are the richer for having heard them. The bloodied conquerors of history, like the fabled Alexander, changed the face of the world:

but how did they make men's lives and souls better?

Now Yeshua is dead, the fount of his words forever stopped. Perhaps now he will be forgotten. But he would be the first to say that it does not matter if his name is forgotten, as long as his ideas live on. And live on they shall. In my long life I have already seen them spreading through the world like ripples, to become part of the great ebb and flow of ideas in the Empire of Carthage and even beyond.

What man could hope for a greater legacy?

CHAPTER 34: HARAHASHI

Not many men live here. This land has beauty, but it is the beauty of heat and sand and the bright sun flashing off the water of the sea. A man can live here. He can eke out a living from the sea and even, with careful husbanding of what rain there is, find a sheltered place where fruit and vegetables might grow.

He will never grow rich, not on such thin fare as this. Yet I am happy. I found a wife whom I can love and she bore me children I adore. Here on the edge of the desolate desert we live, love and laugh, as men and women and children have done throughout all the ages of man, wherever they could find a place to support life.

This place was not always the way it is today. Long ago, in the time of the legendary Hannibal the Great and for centuries afterward, the climate was gentler and people lived here on greener shores, under a kinder sun and more frequent rains. Hannibal himself may even have had a home in these parts, though no one has ever been able to prove such tales true. And truly, more places make claim to him than he could possibly have lived in had he spent his entire life traveling from one to another.

But perhaps... perhaps... I have always dreamt that one day I might be the one to find something from those long past days, buried for centuries beneath the ever shifting sands. Sometimes I will find the remains of a building. Sometimes all that is left are stones, but if I am lucky there might be marble or some other ornamental stone remaining. If I can I will cart these home, for my wife is a talented carver of stone. Occasionally I have even found minor treasures: a well preserved pot, a silver plate, once even some fine gold jewelry. I look at these things and wonder about the people who had owned them: once living, breathing people; now long forgotten, these possessions or treasures of theirs the only, lonely witnesses to their existence. Perhaps my own ancestors are among them, and I wonder if their shades feel the connection when I hold what once was theirs in my own living hands; if they look on in pride or revulsion at what their line has become. I am not a great man, not an especially good man, but nor am I a bad man. I make my own way in the world, and is not that the measure of any man? From the greatest to the least, can the gods ask more of us than that we use what gifts we have to make more than we take, and thus leave the world a richer place than we found it? So whoever my ancestors were, whether a humble potter or the man who gave gold jewelry to his wife or mistress or daughter, if they could see me I believe they would smile and be, if not proud at my magnificence, then at least proud that I am a man.

Occasionally traders ply these shores. They are not great traders, these people, any more than I and my fellow inhabitants are great land owners. If they were they would spurn these unpromising shores unless driven here by storm or emergency. But like me they are what they are and do what they do, and can still eke out their living in the ancient way of our people. If we have had a good crop or catch that is more than we can eat, preserve or trade among our neighbors, these men will take it off my hands for goods or gold, as they will my wife's carvings. And so the treasures I find in the desert find their way to such men, and from there find their way to buyers in realms near and far.

I have a friend among these traders. For a while he was just like any other trader, until one day he said he had a gift for me and asked if I would invite him into my home. Thinking of what tales such a man might tell, and liking him well enough, I was happy to do so. There he opened a small, dark bottle and poured some clear amber liquid into silver goblets.

"Sniff it," he encouraged.

It cleaned out my nose and made my eyes water! It was like some kind of essence of fire had risen out of the liquid. Yet the scent was oddly intoxicating.

"What is that?" I cried.

"Drink it! But only take a sip!"

I looked at him dubiously. He smiled mockingly and tossed his entire ration down his throat in one go, so ignoring his warning I closed my eyes and did the same.

"Baal's toenails!" I cried when I finished choking and coughing, though it is possible I referred to a different part of the god's anatomy. "You have poisoned me!"

"No, no, my friend. You see I am unharmed! Would you like another?"

I surprised myself by thrusting my cup out to him. This time I was more careful. It was like nothing I had ever drunk before.

"What is this? Where did it come from?"

"It is a new invention, or at least new to these parts. Those who trade it will not tell me how they make it, only that they have learned how to purify the very essence of wine. To that I can attest. You know the effect of wine. I assure you, my friend, if I gave you much more than this you would be lying under the table, long before this bottle is empty! I know! I've been there!"

We are an empirical people, and soon I too could attest to its power.

This became our tradition whenever the trader, whose name is Chaeronis, visited. Perhaps we became friends because he saw in me a kindred soul. More likely, one of the pieces I had sold him had proved to be worth far more than he had paid me for it, and out of debt or guilt he brought me his unique gift. Or even more likely, he hoped that where there was one such treasure there might be more, and he wanted to be the one to get them.

I did not begrudge him his profit. Why would I? If I was happy to receive his payment, I was happy, and his good fortune did not negate mine. I liked him, and his friendship seemed no less genuine for being good business as well. But I learned to recognize the glint in his eyes when something I showed him was of especial interest to him, and I bargained accordingly. This game too became a tradition of our friendship. Whether it was his motive or not, while I will trade our other goods with the first merchant to call, I always keep my most interesting pieces for his visits.

For the last two days the weather here was wild, with howling winds from the sea bringing rain that fought with the sand for the pleasure of striking anyone foolish or unlucky enough to be outside. Today the wind has died down to a more gentle breeze and the air is pleasantly cool.

There is not much to find in the desolate places. It is not as if one day people lived here in all their industry and gaiety and then the next they were gone, leaving troves of abandoned goods behind them. No, the loss of water and life and the invasion of the hot sands was a long process, ebbing and flowing until finally the sands declared their victory and only people like me remained. So as the waters and crops ebbed so did the inhabitants, taking all of value with them. Anything that might have been abandoned was picked over by their more persistent neighbors.

A man could spend his life here digging for remains, but if he found the foundations of a house he should not immediately dance with joy, for there may well be nothing left besides those foundations. Whatever remains to be found is the lost or the hidden, and no plan or program of excavation is going to find it. So I wander, and look, and hope, for that is all I can do unless I somehow gained the vision to peer beneath the sands.

That is why today I head out with two camels into the desert, for who knows what those howling winds have revealed? They can move in a day what a man could not move in a lifetime of labor, so truly they are a gift from the gods.

An old building, or what rubble remains of it, has been freed from the dunes after who knows how many centuries. Next to what would once have been a wall, a slab of stone lies flat on the ground. My heart leaps, for from the form of the wall I think the slab once lay beneath the soil of a garden, soil long gone to dust and sand, and now at last blown away. Why would someone put a slab under the ground except to hide something? Why would they hide something unless it was of great value? So I free its edges from the last grip of the ground and with much effort manage to slide it away, revealing a square stone well now filled with fine sand.

Carefully, I begin to dig, until my spade strikes something hard. Even more carefully, I remove the sand from around it, revealing a bronze chest! My head fills with images of gold and jewels and my heart pounds in anticipation, but I tell myself to be calm. Even if it once contained treasure, the owners may have fled with it, leaving just this heavy chest behind. Finally I free the chest and lift it out of its grave. Hands shaking, I break the last remains of a lock and, eyes shut in hope or fear, lever open its lid. I open my eyes and behold... lead pipes!

I frown. Who would hide lead pipes? Then I notice that their ends are closed and I frown again. Lifting one up, I prize off its cap and peer inside. It contains a scroll! I look at the other pipes. This must be a collection of scrolls!

Gingerly, I touch the edge of the exposed scroll with my finger; it bends a little before breaking, though it feels fragile and I dare not try to remove it. Who knows what it contains? I load my find and head home, my mind alive with speculation. I do not know what value old scrolls can have, but I know there are men who care about such ancient knowledge, and perhaps these will prove more valuable than jewels.

~~~

Fortunately for my nerves, it is only a month after my discovery of the scrolls before my friend Chaeronis again reaches our shore and I spy his cheery face approaching. Truth be told my nerves would probably have made me jump at the first trader to arrive, but I am glad it is my friend.

"Greetings, Harahashi my friend! Will you welcome a poor traveler?"

"It is my honor, Chaeronis! Come in, come in! I have something to show you!"

So much for my plan of remaining calm and offhandedly revealing my secret later.

"Oh? If you are too impatient to even drink with me first, it must be something of great value!"

"It is," I assure him, and thus our haggling begins with this warning that I do not expect a cheap offer.

I say no more as I bring him the chest, open it, withdraw the pipe I had already opened, and remove its cap to reveal its contents.

"A scroll?" he says with a frown. "That is your treasure? I fear you may be disappointed in my offer, despite our friendship."

"Not just a scroll! Many scrolls, hidden in a buried chest by the ancients! Who knows, perhaps by Hannibal himself!"

"You would make a fine tout in the market, friend, with lines like that!" he replies with a laugh. "What are they? Do you know?"

"No. I have been afraid to do anything with them, in fear that they would turn to dust under my hands."

"A wise precaution. Have you touched them?"

"I have, gently. Here. See."

Carefully he prods the end with his finger. "Hmmm. Yes. Old parchment, if I am not mistaken, not papyrus. That is good. Both because it is less likely to fall apart and because its contents are likely to be valuable if its owner chose to use it."

Then he remembers himself and shrugs. "Well, if it has any value at all, of course."

He rubs his hands briskly together. "An interesting find, yes, my friend. You were wise to bring it to me. I am sure it will be worth something!" He holds up a finger in caution. "Not necessarily a lot, for what value really lies in old parchments? But there are men who are interested in such things. Historians. Philosophers. Those who study the ancient ways for whatever reason. Come, let us think on it and drink on it, while I consider what may be a fair price."

"No."

"No? Do you refuse my drink, or my trade?"

"Something in these scrolls calls to me. I do not wish to sell them to you. I wish to travel with you, to meet these philosophers of whom you speak and see what they can tell me. And what they will pay me."

He rubs his chin dubiously. "I see. But I know you are not a wealthy man. You cannot afford the price of passage on my ship. You are my friend, but I too must eat."

"Unless you also found a cache of gold coins with your scrolls?" he adds hopefully.

"I will pay you one part in ten of the price I receive for my scrolls."

"One part in ten! The journey will be long, I must provide food and lodging, and at the end the price is uncertain! No, my friend. Half! If the price is high, we will both be wealthy. If the price is low, at least I get some of my costs back."

"You said yourself they must be valuable, being written on parchment. One part in five."

"Valuable to the writer, my friend! For all we know they are the accounts from his auction house, or the bad poetry of a lonely old man, a treasure to his own heart but of no interest to anyone else living or dead! Two parts in five!"

"It is out my friendship to you that I offer you this, but there are other traders. I think you suspect their true value. One third. One third and we can go on this adventure together!"

"When my wife hears of this she will mock me and not sleep with me for a month! You break my heart! But I do not wish to see you offer your scrolls to another and, broken, receive even less, as you surely would! Done!"

We clasp hands, and celebrate our future with his burning wine.

CHAPTER 35: APOLLINARIS

O thers have always thought me strange. Most men, and most women for that matter, focus on their lives, their ambitions, and the other people around them; gaining their strength and meaning from the quality of their food and lodgings and, even more than that, the opinions of their fellows.

I have never cared. Well, obviously I care to eat and to have shelter, and I even gain pleasure from having those better rather than worse. He who was the first of the ancient Greek philosophers, the great Thales of Miletus, told us to know ourselves. And I know that food and shelter are necessary for life and that enjoyment and pleasure are necessary to make life worth living. I even enjoy the company of women, and indeed there is one, a courtesan and in her way as strange as I, with whom I share both friendship and bed. In a tale related by the great philosopher Plato, the playwright Aristophanes imagined that in our primal state men and women were unified spherical beings, for what is a more perfect form than the sphere? Then we were split asunder, and ever after we have sought the union we once had, and poor as the attempt is, in our closest approach to it we may achieve our greatest bliss. Though it must be said, from my observations, the mating of man and woman with its tangle of bodies and limbs is as little like a sphere as I can imagine.

But I digress. That too is part of my oddness, I suppose. For whenever my mind sees an idea it cannot resist chasing it down its burrow like a ferret after a rabbit, not giving up until the idea is taken and digested or, more rarely, forever lost in the twists and turns of logic. Thus my mind is something like a tree, constantly filling out branches down to their twigs and leaves, then returning to continue where it left off. And while some twigs remain barren the tree itself flourishes, and so my understanding grows.

I was speaking of my oddness. All boys growing up have their enemies. Like play, their friendships and enmities presage the more serious versions they will face in their adult lives. Yet despite my oddness I had few serious problems growing up. Boys often do not like those who are better than they are, unless it is at sport, which engenders admiration rather than scorn. But I was always an inoffensive lad, and if I knew my mind was greater than others' it was simply a datum, like my sex and height, and it did not cause me to look down on anyone. Indeed, I was both inoffensive and always willing to help when asked, and so as I grew older my enemies fell in number and most of my fellows came to regard me with something approaching warmth, even if they did speak of me sometimes as a mysterious being they would never understand.

There, I have digressed again. I spoke of Thales, and he was a man I admire. Too many of the philosophers who followed him, for all their wisdom in matters of the mind are less practical in matters of daily living. Thales was both philosopher and businessman: thinker and doer. He knew himself better than most, for is that not what we are? Not a mind with in inconvenient body it must satisfy, nor a body with an inconvenient mind to nag it about its desires, but a unified being of both? Perhaps achieving that unity of mind and body in its true perfection is the real finality we should be seeking.

And so I too am a practical man. When I can, I use the knowledge I acquire to bring into the world new things to ease the lives of men. Sometimes these are spurned. But enough have met with favor that I am a wealthy man. I use my wealth to learn more, gathering knowledge from the far corners of the world. For wisdom is the thing I value most. Do you think Apollinaris is the name I was born with? No, it is the name I myself chose in honor of the god Apollo. Like most gods he is god of many things, but primarily things of the mind, and mostly truth and light. What my name was does not matter. For surely what we choose is more important, and more our measure, than the accidents with which we are born.

But for all my wisdom I know something is missing, the sphere of my ideal nature not yet perfected. I see clues to it, hints, but as yet my mental ferret remains hungry. Plato is the philosopher whom most of the wise men of the world follow. I can see why. The breadth of his vision and the seduction of his thought show him to be one of the great minds of history. Yet there is something unsatisfying about his vision of a world where true knowledge and the material world exist in separate realms, the second inferior to the first. For do we not all live and breathe in that material world? Thus I am more partial to the greatest of his students, Aristotle. He knew how to look at the real world, and the breadth of his accomplishments is staggering: plants, animals, ethics, politics, poetry; few disciplines of thought escaped his penetrating gaze. Yet while his practical knowledge is revered and used by all, most men are too far beneath him. Thus they see his words but not his methods: neither knowing nor caring that how he gained this knowledge is more important than the knowledge itself. And so they use his gifts like revelations passed down from the gods: something to stare at as if from another realm, to be taken and not questioned.

Now will you understand my tale? My hunger for knowledge is as well-known as my wealth. And so it is that men bring me unusual animals and plants and mysterious artifacts from far lands or times. And so it is that at the end of one strand of the silken net I have cast across the world dangles a minor trader named Chaeronis. And so it is that one day he arrived here with a rough desert dweller of the name Harahashi. Now I will tell their tale.

They brought to me a bronze chest, inside of which were twenty sealed lead pipes. One had been opened and inside it was an ancient scroll of parchment.

I bade them stay as my guests, for I could not offer a fair price until I had determined their nature; and besides I enjoyed both Chaeronis' tales of his travels and this unique opportunity to learn about the lives of the desert dwellers. Over the next few days I extracted the scroll and carefully unwound it on a long bench, covering it with sheets of glass as I did. I did not attempt to read it as I did so, not wishing to distract myself. Instead I merely unwound it as a mechanical puzzle, savoring the anticipation of being able to read the whole once it was ready.

One of my recent inventions is to grind pure glass into a curved shape which magnifies objects under it. The idea had come to me after observing the distortions caused by the ripples in glass sheets, some of which seemed to make the background appear larger. No doubt many before me have seen this curious effect. But Aristotle taught me the value of close observation and more, the virtue of thinking about what it means. I did not know what it meant, but it inspired an idea. If ripples in flawed glass magnify objects imperfectly, might the perfection of a sphere magnify them perfectly? And so I experimented with grinding glass, discovering that a flattened sphere did indeed allow me to see tiny things in their perfection of form. An ant can be a fearsome creature indeed when viewed in this way! I have only just started down this particular burrow, and wonder what other marvels lie at its end. But for now, my simple enlarging glass itself is valuable in examining this scroll resurrected from the past, for many parts are faded or damaged.

When I understood what I had, I called my guests to view it.

"Your scroll is remarkable! It is a historical record, though an unusual one. It is not all about major historical events like kings and wars, though they are alluded to. Its main purpose appears to be to record the daily lives and beliefs of the general citizenry of the ancient Carthaginians. From the language, which is Greek of the dialect current around the time of Carthage's wars with Rome, and the kinds of things recorded, it purports to have been written around the time of Hannibal the Great. I do not know how much new knowledge we will gain from it, but I dare say an extensive personal record from that time will be of great interest to many even without new revelations. If this were the war memoirs of Hannibal himself, it would be worth a fortune. Sadly, it is much more prosaic fare.

"Now. That is just this one scroll. Perhaps the others have less value. Perhaps they have more. I do not think you wish to stay here idly while I carefully open them all and divine their contents."

I was keen to own these scrolls and I did not want these men to look elsewhere for another buyer. So I offered them a sum. You do not need to know the sum. It was double what the scrolls would be worth if they were all the same as the one we could see. As I explained to them, this was in case one of them proved to be of more significance, but it was most likely they were all of a similar nature.

They looked at each other, and without great urgency attempted to bargain up the price. I knew they would have accepted my original offer but we settled on half again as much. At the time I chided myself that I had paid too much, but the more I thought about these scrolls the more I knew I wanted them. And which buyer does not feel he has paid too much, and which seller does not feel the opposite? But now... now I feel a twinge of guilt, for paying them too little.

I had noticed that carved into each pipe was a symbol, and it did not take me long to deduce that these were numbers in the Greek system. The scroll we had started with was therefore the third.

Having solved this minor puzzle, I set myself the task of deciphering my new library in the proper order, and it appeared to be what I had told my guests.

Do you wonder why I now feel guilt at the price?

It began when I was half way through the fifth scroll, for I had long since abandoned my earlier policy of waiting until the whole was revealed. I came across a long section of text around which the author had drawn a decorative border. This puzzled me, for until then it was all plain text, as if the writer believed his unadorned words were treasure enough, and there was nothing special about the content it framed. Perhaps the author had simply been bored, and decided to decorate his manuscript?

But then the border ended and a repeat of its design started. But what lay within was not the archaic Greek of the rest. It was in an unknown language, not just the words but the alphabet! The letters were strange, many the same or at least similar to the Latin alphabet of the Romans, but overall like no language I had seen before.

I gasped, as the meaning of the decorative borders became clear. A translation! A key to this strange new language! But why? With trembling hands I continued to unroll the scroll, wondering what mysteries I might find. But then the border came to an end and what followed was but a continuation of the original story in Greek.

I stared at it, puzzled. What is the point of including a key to a new language that tells nothing new and does not continue? And why here, dropped seemingly at random into the middle of this scroll? Then I glanced over at the next scroll, still nestled in its leaden crypt, and I began to be tremble again, though I do not know whether I was more afraid of what I would find or what I would not.

I did not have enough mental ferrets to chase all the rabbits who were hopping about. I would impose the order of my mind on my unruly emotions. Perhaps the crucial answers lay further within the current scroll. Demanding ferrets or no, I must see this task to its proper end and order, for as much as spontaneous inspiration has its own brilliance, it should not come at the expense of sound method.

But the manuscript just continued as it had. Then at last I opened the next scroll and began to reveal its contents. At first I was disappointed, for it was just more of the same handwriting in the same archaic Greek. But when I translated the words, I gasped. For this is what I read:

> I am Angela Milton, wife of Hannibal the son of
> Hamilcar Barca of Carthage. This is my story.

I sat down, stunned, my earlier words echoing in my mind. *If this were the war memoirs of Hannibal himself, it would be worth a fortune.* By all the gods! Everyone knows the tales of Hannibal's wife, called the Witch of Carthage by her enemies. That she was a foreigner, supposedly from Spain, but her true origins were obscure. As obscure as the wild legends of her powers over water and fire, life and death, were unlikely. She was a shadowy figure even in her own time, as much reviled as revered, with some claiming her dark powers held Hannibal if not all of Carthage in her thrall. Yet after the war she did surprisingly little for one so puissant, and other than some wild myths about her part in the fabled First Fleet to Amerika, she led a quiet life without obvious harm to anyone.

What followed this stunning introduction was in the unknown language.

I stopped to pore over this new text and what it might mean. Was this truly written by Hannibal's wife, a woman even more steeped in myth than Hannibal himself? But if she wished to tell her story, why introduce it in Greek then write it in a language nobody knew? Who was it for? Her own people? Who were they? Had there been some higher civilization in the far north, lost even in the time of Hannibal, and this woman its last refugee? But if so, why would they use a derivative of the Latin alphabet? And who did she think would there be to read it?

I continued to carefully unroll the scroll, and as I did I discovered it contained four sections. First was the brief introduction. Then came some inches of writing in that strange language. Then she returned to a similar short passage in Greek, though its content was disappointing: just a rather stilted account of her observations of Carthage. The rest of the scroll then resumed in the new language.

I pondered what all this meant. Had she known that those who found her legacy might not know her language, and therefore left them a key to unlock her meaning? But why two keys, assuming that is what I had found? Had she thought her words so important that she even left a second, shorter key, in case the first was lost? But if that was her motive, why use the other language at all?

It was as if she desperately wanted her message to be understood, yet equally desperately tried to hide it. And then buried it.

It is her message, not to the people of her own time, but to the future!

How right I was, yet how staggeringly wrong.

And so I set myself to understanding the keys to her secret language and translating her tale. And I continued to open her scrolls, wondering what other treasures might lie within.

~~~

So now here I sit before my fire, warming my feet with its flames and my stomach with the burning liquor Chaeronis left me when we sealed the deal that will change my life forever.

I have opened all the scrolls now. Most were her depiction of Carthage and her observations of its people and the various tribes she encountered on her journeys with Hannibal. A tale she had continued even after the day she was struck with the sudden desire to tell her own story as well. As if she imagined that her original task had any importance next to the far brighter diamond she buried within it!

For the past year I have devoted myself to translating her story, aided not only by her keys but by her habit of occasionally adding a little box wherein she would put some extra definitions or explanations. Still there are parts I am uncertain of, some words whose meaning eludes me, but I am sure I have its essence.

Am I mad? Or was she?

For she was Angela Milton, wife of Hannibal, and this is her story.

She says she came from a far future, thousands of years after Hannibal's time. In her future it was Rome who had become the great empire, leaving Carthage in ruins. How she travelled in time she could not say: all she knew was she had been hurled back into the past by a storm.

But staggering as that is, it is not what leaves my mind spinning the most. For I have seen a different future, one shining a light on what our own future may become. In explaining her world she reveals that it is ruled by a thing she calls 'science'. This is a new way of knowing: not Plato looking inward, sitting in his cave and imagining shadows, nor even Aristotle looking at what is in the world outside. It is the fusion of both these great men with the practicality of Thales, as if in culmination of the myth of our eternal quest to regain our primordial perfection. As if these three finally merged into a perfected sphere of philosophy: of mind, senses and action. The careful observer and empirical thinker, Aristotle, coupled with the abstract thinker, Plato, energized by the doer, Thales. Not merely looking, not merely thinking: but having thought, then testing the consequences of that thought. Not content to passively look at the world, not content to limit one's actions to spinning tales in one's head, but actively poking at the world to see how it pushes back. Not only describing; not stopping at a plausible explanation; but saying 'here is what I think, and if I am right and I do *this,* then *that* will happen.' Then *doing* it, and thereby knowing whether our thoughts are true or false! And continuing to do this, observation after observation, thought after thought, test after test, until all the secrets of the world are laid bare before us!

I take a drink to feel the fire burn its way down my throat, and wonder whether I will wake to find this revelation but a dream.

But she was no goddess, this Angela, no heavenly being whose vision transcended time and space and who gazed at the pain of men with Olympian detachment. Just a woman, if not like any other, then subject to the same doubts, uncertainty and pain that all of us must face.

If her enemies wished her ill, they would have been glad to see into her mind. She helped Carthage, she wrote, because for all its grandeur Rome was an empire of the sword, and its legacy of blood still reverberated even to her own time. As an empire of trade, she thought, surely Carthage would do better. But for all Rome's flaws, she knew what greatness it had still reached and that she would destroy, and the knowledge ate away at her soul.

I hope that in the end she found peace.

For in her torment she gave me another clue. For she described the history of her world.

And for all its flaws and dark ages, her history seems to have been a more vibrant and active one than ours: its reversals compensated by periods of shining progress, until in the last and greatest of its rebirths her 'science' was invented and transformed her world. In our world, our people have grown fat and content. We are wealthy, and for the most part peace rules the world. Yes, there have been times when for many reasons darkness would eat at the edges of our empire, even reach toward its heart. But we were always too strong, always too widespread, for these to be more than annoyances to be crushed in the course of time.

In her world there was more struggle; more fiercely independent nation states contending to extend their dominion or merely survive against such invaders. Perhaps that was its spark, the spark that finally ignited science: the need to survive, the will to prosper, the demands to be better than your neighbors or vanish from the Earth. Perhaps there can be too much peace, too much contentment, where the need to improve may be even less than the comfort of stability. It isn't that we have not improved over the centuries since this woman wrote her tale; but perhaps not as much as she hoped; perhaps she brought us peace, but at the expense of progress.

Had she known, would she have chosen differently? Would I? I am glad I do not face that choice. Who could bear the weight of it? To choose between the deaths of so many or the stagnation of the human race?

I raise my cup in silent salute to the flames and this woman of centuries past and centuries to come. *How did you bear it? You cannot hear me, Angela, but I honor your courage. And if you could hear my thoughts, I would tell you this: you did what you thought was right, and who can do better?*

I smile in mockery at my own thoughts, as I can hardly be an impartial judge in this matter. For surely I myself would not exist if she hadn't done what she did, and who does not love their own life above all things? Nothing can escape causality and consequence, not even the gods. I think of the people who died because of her, and their children who were never born. The people who lived, and their children who never had been before. The Roman soldiers who never marched into foreign lands, and the Phoenician traders who did. In places more central or cosmopolitan, those consequences might have taken mere years or decades to manifest. In other places, more distant, isolated or insular, perhaps centuries would pass before those who once had lived would live no longer, with strangers living in their stead. And not merely living in their stead, like interchangeable chips in a game; but each a living, thinking, unique person with their own talents, loves and dreams. How long will it be before those ripples spread to cover the whole world? Perhaps they already have.

But this is my age; and now I know the truth. I know the secret, and perhaps when we reach the time she would have been born, our society will yet overtake hers in glory. I smile to myself. My people have grown fat, yes, and they lack the whips of war to drive them into new realms of thought. But one thing they care about is wealth, and what will my people do once they learn the power of science to create it? Today is one of the cusps on which the history of the world turns, a flag falling to start our ultimate race. A race to decide which is truly the greater spur to creation, if only we had known there was a choice to be made or a race to be run. Steel and blood? Or gold and life?

I will not tell the world what I have found. No, they would not believe, and in their disbelief they would spurn the greater truth. So I will not tell, I will simply do. I will develop the clues Hannibal's Witch left me. I will found my own school, a school of science, and attract here all people of independent and penetrating thought. And the fruits of our science will show the world its truth.

She buried her work in the hope that a future age would find it. I shall bury it again for yet another generation to find. Then after men have learned the truth of science, one day they will know the truth of how it came to be born into our world.

Again I raise my cup to the flames.

Goodbye, Angela Milton. You left your legacy to the future, and if I succeed it will be a greater legacy than you could have imagined. Do men's souls live on after death, as some say? I hope so, and that wherever you are you see what you have achieved, and feel pride in your most singular life.

Chapter 36: Angela

I wake up in a delightfully soft bed.

This puzzles me.

Am I still alive, or is this the now never-to-be-written Hamlet's dream, those dreams that follow death, from which we may never wake?

As dreams go, this one isn't too bad. The bed is luxuriantly soft, the sheet that drapes my naked body the same. I run my hands over my body then freeze. There is something weird about it, and it takes me a moment to realize what it is. I touch my breasts, feeling their smooth skin stretched over their soft fullness. My hands dart to my face. Smooth. The face of a young woman.

I shriek, and sit up.

"What is it?" comes a sleepy voice, a man's voice, from beside me. The voice is as strange to me as my body, for it is not Hannibal's, when for decades now no other man would dare sleep in my bed.

I shriek, louder this time, and jump entirely out of bed.

I remember I am naked and grab the sheet to cover myself, turning the shriek up yet another notch. Alas, my sheet-grabbing uncovers him as effectively as it covers me, and you will be unsurprised to learn that upon seeing his unfamiliar nakedness lying there, my trend of shrieks is showing no signs of abating.

My eyes finally make it to his face, which is staring at me as if I have gone mad, and it is as if the decades fall away. Even the shrieks can't cope with this and they give up in mid cry. I merely gasp, staring at him with an equal mix of incomprehension and terror.

Ricky? I think.

"Ricky?" I cry.

"Were you expecting someone else?" he asks. As if I'm the crazy one.

"I… I… I…" I stutter articulately. Then I give up entirely, and just stare at him.

"Too much tequila?"

"Tequila?"

"That drink you had a lot of. We had a lot of."

"Drink?"

"Are you OK, Angela?"

"OK?"

I look at him helplessly. So it was all a dream? I think back to the dream. *Forty years' worth? What was in that tequila?*

I think more about the dream. How could any dream pack in that much detail? Whenever I try to recall something, from the day I awoke in old Carthage to the night I walked out into the storm, I can recall it: in a rich sensory tapestry, not in the vague and surreal way a normal dream presents itself in the light of day. Yet here I am, and here he is, and what the hell? I've heard that time can be compressed in dreams, even if it is only your mind back-filling context when you wake. But this is insane.

"I… I just had the weirdest dream. Ever."

"No, it's all true. You are a bitcoin millionaire, you are attending a celebration filled with tequila and sashimi, and we spent the night together in your room."

I look at him helplessly. "I know all that! I think! But that was *forty years ago! How could I have forty years' worth of dream!"* I feel my voice rising toward hysteria—perhaps beyond—and stop.

"I'm sure if you describe it to me you will realize it was only a dream."

"Yeah… yeah, I guess so. But it seemed so real! More real than… last night? Was it really only last night!?"

"You don't look forty years older to me, Angela."

I touch my face again. "Yes… yes, there is that. But the last time I looked at my face, I was old! Old!!!" I take a deep breath. "But it seemed so real…"

He smiles. "So what was this amazing dream about?"

I try to pretend I am sane. That I too know it was a dream.

"I guess it was just prompted by all that talk… last night. About the Phoenicians. I dreamed I woke up in Old Carthage! That I met Hannibal! For Christ's sake, Ricky, I *married* Hannibal! And… I used my knowledge to help him. It wasn't Carthage that was destroyed, but Rome that was stopped! And I sent them to America! Because I knew it was there! And when I… left… Ricky! I died! By the time I left, Carthage was ascendant, the greatest empire in the world!"

"So, how was he?"

"What?"

"In the sack. Hannibal. Any good?"

Typical man. All that, and that is his take-away. At least he refrained from waving at his own parts to invite *that* comparison. "*Ricky!* I'm serious!"

He laughs, and I grind my teeth. "Look, it might be funny to you, but do I look like I'm laughing?" I shiver and hug myself, then pause. That's odd…

"Ricky… do you remember this scar on my arm?" I clearly remember how I got it: in a fall at sea when I gashed my arm. In Phoenicia over two millennia ago, not in my life here.

He looks at it. "No, no, I don't remember it. But it is quite a fine scar. I was a bit distracted…"

I shiver. What does this mean? Could it be that only a few hours have passed here, so my body is young; yet it retains the scars of those forty years, a literal physical embodiment of the years carved into my flesh, as my memories of them are still burned into my brain? Thank the gods I didn't lose a leg or something. Though at least that would have wiped the grin off Ricky's damn face.

Lose a leg or something…

"Ricky… do you remember the story about Hannibal losing an eye when he crossed into Italy?"

"Yes, of course. It is well known."

"That is something else I changed. I saved his eye."

"Busy girl."

"I had forty years!"

"Right…"

"Can you do me a favor? Besides wiping that smirk off your effing face?"

I admit the smirk is annoying me. I'm not sure whether knowing how crazy I sound makes the smirk more or less irritating.

"Look it up," I explain.

"Look it up?"

"Is there an echo in here? Look it up on the web. Humor me. See if he lost an eye or not."

His smirk returns, not that it had ever really gone. "You want me to find out if he kept his eye? Not, say, something trivial like the complete absence of the Roman Empire?"

"Baby steps. I thought I'd start small and work my way up." I admit it had sounded more reasonable when I was thinking it.

He lifts his eyebrow at my lame explanation. I have the grace to blush, knowing I deserve it, but then he kindly explains the meaning of the eyebrow as if I'm an idiot or something. "You know this is crazy, right?"

I sigh. "Yes, Ricky, I retain enough common sense to know it is crazy. But you weren't there. It was so *real!* I just need to know!"

He shrugs, reaches for his phone and starts tapping on it. His smirk changes to a puzzled frown. "That's odd…"

"WHAT? … I mean, what?"

"No service. Weird. There was no problem last night. Maybe the cell network is down."

"Surely you can't have a building full of billionaire geeks and not have wifi!"

He nods and taps. "Huh. No wifi either. Doubly weird. Not even anyone's phone offering a hotspot. The storm maybe?"

"Maybe it's your phone."

"Yeah. Where's yours?"

I look around and spy it lying by the bed. I imagine clothes and phones flying every which way last night, and decide that remaining naked under those circumstances is just too distracting. "First things first, lover boy. Time to get dressed."

He looks about to object, but one look in my eyes reminds him of the proverb about discretion and valor, and we both hurriedly dress. Then I fetch my phone and turn it on.

"Here we are. Let me try. Ah! No phone service but I get wifi. Oh…"

"What?"

"Just one idiot's hotspot. Someone called 'Ricky'."

We stare at each other, nonplussed. Then I look around the room.

"Um, Ricky, does this place look right to you?"

He looks around. "Well I wasn't paying much attention to the décor. But yeah... now you mention it. It seems... smaller. And... different somehow."

"Like... wasn't there a window over there?"

"And... where's the door?"

"Am I still dreaming, Ricky?"

At least his smirk has packed up and gone home. He stares at the wall and shrugs. "Well, since it's Crazy Hour, let me try something."

He walks slowly toward a blank spot of wall. As he approaches, he reaches out to it and it vanishes. It now opens upon a balcony, garlanded with flowering vines. Not an image of a balcony. An actual, real balcony, complete with pleasant breeze.

He turns to look at me, his eyes wide. His mouth opens and shuts a few times, but seems unable to decide on any words to utter. He reaches his hand out to me.

I join him on the balcony, nicely private here but curving around a corner. I look at that corner, unaccountably afraid, and now squeeze his hand more firmly, hoping to draw some strength or sanity from his touch. "Let's take a look at the view," I suggest shakily. He nods, still dumb, and we walk around the corner to a view of the city and sea.

The sea is still there, but the city is gone. Another city lives in its place. A city of tall crystal spires, shining like a city of light. Points of light like multicolored fireflies dart among the towers, while other points of light join into aerial streams flowing into and out of the city. Occasionally larger lights shoot up into the sky, as if heading out into space itself.

We look at the scene for long minutes.

"Ricky... are you seeing this?"

"If you mean am I seeing some city out of the Wizard of Oz, yes."

"If I'm still dreaming, why are you in my dream?"

"I don't feel like a figment of your imagination."

"OW!" The swine pinched me hard on the bottom.

"Sorry, just performing standard diagnostic tests." At least he has the decency to give himself a similar pinch.

"If this is real, then same question. What are you doing here? If everything else has changed, why are *you* still here? For that matter, how are we still in a hotel?"

He gets a distant look in his eyes. "I suppose... we were together." Then he starts rabbiting on about virtual futures, possible quantum entanglement of potentialities and bubbles of alternative existences stretching to accommodate each other. Either he's read more Einstein than I have or he's making it up as he goes along.

"Shut up, Ricky."

He shuts up.

"For that matter, if this is some advanced civilization, why don't our phones work?"

He looks at me with a peculiar intensity. "Unfortunately... or depending on how you look at it, fortunately... that one is easier. Network frequencies and protocols are all very logical and based on physical laws, but the details are pretty much arbitrary. Whatever these people use for communications, it isn't going to be compatible with what we had. Even if the frequencies are identical the protocols will never connect."

Apparently he's read more electrical engineering than me, too.

My hand seeks out his again, and we stand there together, staring at a new world.

"What are we going to do now, Ricky?" I whisper.

"Bug out, before hotel management turn up demanding payment in silver shekels or something?"

I laugh. Unfortunately, he has a point.

We start walking toward the city. As we walk, I notice he is fiddling with his phone, and I understand why when a song begins to waft from his phone into the predawn night, a female voice singing from another age, "If I could turn back time..."

I lean my head on his shoulder as we walk. "What are we going to do, about... anything? Yesterday we were millionaires. Now we have no money, no jobs, no knowledge, no language."

"What people have always done. What we must."

We crest a rise and stand looking at the city. *We are the New Phoenicians.* "That city," I say softly. "I made it, didn't I?"

He looks at me, his expression suddenly grave, and he replies with a calm certainty I do not understand.

"Yes."

"It looks... magnificent. But how do we know all that glitter isn't an illusion? A palace built on the blood and sweat of serfs? So when we look from afar all we see is the glory, but up close we will find the lights are just a few princes of this world, lifted on the broken bodies of millions crushed beneath their boots?"

"I don't think so. You don't get a city like that without science, technology and wealth. In our time those were the great levelers, which raised the millions out of poverty for the first time. They are what brought freedom to the world and put an end to the princes."

But now at last as the shock of my rebirth recedes, it is replaced by my horror at what I did to make that city. I find myself too weak to stand, and collapse onto a nearby rock. "But at what cost?" I whisper. "Our world. The world we knew. They are all dead. I have killed them all!"

I look up at him. "And why am I alive? Why did they have to bring me back? Why couldn't they just let me die?!"

Then I too would be dead, beyond guilt and pain and consequence. And perhaps that is why.

He reaches his hands to me and raises me to my feet, his dark eyes staring into mine. Then he speaks to me and it is as if some strange strength is flowing into me from my hands, and his words have the power to soothe away my guilt.

"But look at it another way. All the people there, all the people on Earth today: you gave them life. They would not exist without you. You have not killed anyone, but rather changed who is alive."

"Is that enough to pay for what I have done?" I whisper, the shadow of my guilt refusing to release me so easily. "Can anything ever be enough?"

"Ask them."

Then we both turn, and stand together gazing into the distance, my hand still drawing comfort from his. The edge of the sun rises above the waves, scattering its pink light onto the clouds, flashing off the gleaming walls of the city and its firefly host of aircraft.

I wonder if it will all still be here tomorrow. Or like the world I once knew, will it too disappear like the mist of a dream?

I grip Ricky's hand more tightly, as if the touch of another's living flesh might help anchor me to reality. I turn my head and lift my eyes to his face, but he is not looking at me. He is looking at the distant sight, with a smile that cannot decide whether to be happy or sad, and I wonder whether the vista he stares at is the city or the future. Then as I gaze at his face and wonder what he is seeing, it is as if I see lightning flickering in his dark eyes.

But I think it is just the lights of the city.

ABOUT THE AUTHOR

Dr Robin Craig has a PhD in molecular biology and a keen interest in science and philosophy. He believes that novels, like all art, should be one in thought, theme and style: to nourish the mind as much as the soul. His books specialize in blending fact and speculation in dramatic and engaging stories, driven by strong characters and intriguing philosophical themes.

In addition to near future science fiction exploring contemporary issues such as artificial intelligence (*Frankensteel*), genetic engineering (*The Geneh War*) and cyborg technology (*Time Enough for Killing*), his books include time travel (*The Time Surgeons* and *Hannibal's Witch*), alternative history (*The Passion of Judas* and *Hannibal's Witch*) and a collection of short stories (*Past, Present, Future*).

He also writes non-fiction. In addition to 14 scientific papers and a long-running philosophical series in *TableAus* (the journal of Australian Mensa), he has published numerous philosophical essays on Amazon.com and was a contributor to *The Australian Book of Atheism* with his chapter *Good Without God*, an essay on the importance and validity of secular ethics.

Dr Craig is an independent author. If you like this book please spread the word with reviews and recommendations to your friends or library... and enjoy more of his books!

To keep up to date on new and upcoming works and events, like his Facebook page: fb.me/authorcraig

www.ingramcontent.com/pod-product-compliance
Lightning Source LLC
Chambersburg PA
CBHW020518120726
47904CB00003B/878